One Hot DADDY

Other Books by Anna Durand

One Hot Chance (Hot Brits, Book One)
One Hot Roomie (Hot Brits, Book Two)
One Hot Crush (Hot Brits, Book Three)
The Dixon Brothers Trilogy (Hot Brits, Books 1-3 + Bonus Chapters)
One Hot Escape (Hot Brits, Book Four)
One Hot Rumor (Hot Brits, Book Five)
One Hot Christmas (Hot Brits, Book Six)
One Hot Scandal (Hot Brits, Book Seven)
One Hot Deal (Hot Brits, Book Eight)
One Hot Favor (Hot Brits, Book Nine)
One Hot Bash (Hot Brits, Book Ten)
One Hot Moment (Hot Brits, Book Eleven)
One Hot Chase (Hot Brits, Book Twelve)
The American Wives Club (A Hot Brits/Hot Scots/Au Naturel Crossover)
Brit vs. Scot (A Hot Brits/Hot Scots/Au Naturel Crossover)
A Novel Secret (A Hot Brits/Hot Scots/Au Naturel Crossover)
The MacTaggart Brothers Trilogy (Hot Scots, Books 1-3)
Gift-Wrapped in a Kilt (Hot Scots, Book Four)
Notorious in a Kilt (Hot Scots, Book Five)
Insatiable in a Kilt (Hot Scots, Book Six)
Lethal in a Kilt (Hot Scots, Book Seven)
Irresistible in a Kilt (Hot Scots, Book Eight)
Devastating in a Kilt (Hot Scots, Book Nine)
Spellbound in a Kilt (Hot Scots, Book Ten)
Relentless in a Kilt (Hot Scots, Book Eleven)
Incendiary in a Kilt (Hot Scots, Book Twelve)
Wild in a Kilt (Hot Scots, Book Thirteen)
Unstoppable in a Kilt (Hot Scots, Book Fourteen)
Valentine in a Kilt (Hot Scots, Book Fifteen)
Electrifying in a Kilt (Hot Scots, Book Sixteen)
The Notorious Dr. MacT (A Hot Scots Prequel)
The British Bastard (A Hot Scots Prequel)
Treachery in the Highlands (A Hot Scots Prequel)
Natural Obsession (Au Naturel Nights, Book One)
Natural Deception (Au Naturel Nights, Book Two)
Naturel Temptation (Au Naturel Nights, Book Three)
The Complete Au Naturel Trilogy, Book Three
Lachlan in a Kilt (The Ballachulish Trilogy, Book One)
Aidan in a Kilt (The Ballachulish Trilogy, Book Two)
Rory in a Kilt (The Ballachulish Trilogy, Book Three)
The Complete Echo Power Trilogy
The Janusite Trilogy (Undercover Elementals, Books 1-3)
Obsidian Hunger (Undercover Elementals, Book Four)
Unbidden Hunger (Undercover Elementals, Book Five)
The Thirteenth Fae (Undercover Elementals, Book Six)
Cyneric (Undercover Elementals, Book Seven)
The Immortal Falls (Undercover Elementals, Book Eight)

One Hot DADDY

Hot Brits, Book Thirteen

ANNA DURAND

JACOBSVILLE BOOKS JB CHESTERHILL, OHIO`

ONE HOT DADDY

ISBN: 978-1-964417-63-9 (paperback)
ISBN: 978-1-964417-64-6 (ebook)
ISBN: 978-1-964417-65-3 (retail audiobook)
ISBN:978-1-964417-66-0 (library audiobook)

Manufactured in the United States.

Jacobsville Books
www.JacobsvilleBooks.com

Publisher's Cataloging-in-Publication Data
provided by Five Rainbows Cataloging Services

Names: Durand, Anna.
Title: One hot daddy / Anna Durand.
Description: Chesterhill, OH : Jacobsville Books, 2025. | Series: Hot Brits, bk. 13.
Identifiers: ISBN 978-1-964417-63-9 (paperback) | ISBN 978-1-964417-64-6 (ebook) | ISBN 978-1-964417-65-3 (retail audiobook) | ISBN 978-1-964417-66-0
Subjects: LCSH: Single fathers--Fiction | Nannies--Fiction. | Man-woman relationships--Fiction. | British--Fiction. | Americans--Fiction. | Romance fiction. | BISAC: FICTION / Romance / Contemporary. | FICTION / Romance / Romantic Comedy. | FICTION / Romance / Small Town & Rural. | FICTION / Romance / Workplace. | GSAFD: Love stories. | Humorous fiction..
Classification: LCC PS3604.U724 O49 2025 (print) | LCC PS3604.U724 (ebook) | DDC 813/.6--dc23.

Chapter One

Fletcher

Ah, what a lovely, sunny morning this is—until I woke up to the dulcet tones of my daughter Amelia shrieking. It's not the "someone's dying" sort. No, it's the "don't you dare change the TV channel" variety. Normally, I rise an hour earlier than the children so I can enjoy a shower and a quiet cup of coffee before I command them to get out of bed. But I had a long night fixing work problems. My job as general manager of the hotel often requires round-the-clock attention.

Unfortunately, I spent three hours fixing the hotel's Wi-Fi network since our tech expert is away on vacation. I didn't get home until midnight.

I'd been about to jump into the shower when the fracas began. So, I hastily pull on a robe and jog into the living room. "What's the problem, Amelia?"

My fifteen-year-old daughter is sitting on the sofa with her arms crossed, chin lifted. "I was watching my favorite show, but Josh stole the remote from me. I had it first."

My oldest son rolls his eyes disdainfully. "You're such a girl."

I'm about to issue an edict when Henry, my eight-year-old son, shuffles into the room. He folds his arms over his chest, much like Amelia had done, and frowns at me. I waste no time on trying to guess what Henry wants. I've learned that in this house, mornings belong to the swift and the shamelessly loud. Henry wanders over to sofa, wearing a t-shirt and no socks, then flops down on the sofa.

I try my best to glower at him. "Henry, shoes *and* socks, please."

"Ugh, Dad, socks make me itchy."

Before I can argue with him about that, my eleven-year-old daughter, Charlotte, emerges from the bedroom she shares with Amelia and ambles past me. Her hair flounces about in wild brown loops, and her shorts barely reach below her hips.

I grasp Charlotte's elbow, halting her. "We've talked about this before, pet. Shorts must cover your thigh down to at least halfway to the knee."

"Come on, Dad," she whines. "I'm not super old like Grandma."

"That's the rule. No exceptions."

My daughter sighs, her shoulders sagging. Then she jogs back to her room, emerging moments later wearing appropriate attire—and holding a soccer ball under one arm.

I kiss her cheek. "Thank you, pet."

She rolls her eyes, then wanders over to the table, balancing that soccer ball on her hip while she pours herself a glass of orange juice. Most of it makes it into the cup. Some, by design, spills onto Henry's bare foot.

"Charlie, you jerk!" he says with all the petulance of an eight-year-old. "I'm telling Dad!"

His sister makes a farting noise with her lips.

"Enough. I *am* Dad, and I'm right here," I declare, setting a hot frying pan on the stove and pretending I didn't just step on a Lego. Henry loves those blasted things.

"Oh no, you're not Dad yet," Amelia declares, not looking up from her juice. "You haven't had your coffee yet. You're super grumpy until then."

She's not wrong. I'm hovering somewhere in the pre-coffee hour, running on muscle memory and adrenaline as I shuffle through the kitchen in mismatched slippers, cracking eggs into the bowl as Henry and Charlotte escalate their dispute into a full-court press.

Charlotte bounces the soccer ball once. "Boys. They're such annoying little babies."

I'm about to intervene when a family mechanical noise starts up. "Henry! Turn off the electric scooter and put it in the closet."

"Where's the food? I'm starving to death."

"You'll get breakfast if you put your arse in a chair."

Josh's eyes bulge, and his jaw drops in fake shock. "Dad just used a bad word."

Charlotte apes her brother's expression. "Ooh, what word?"

He leans forward to stage whisper, "A-R-S-E."

Oh, bollocks. I never use rude language in front of my children, but I just can't seem to get my head on straight this morning.

I slop eggs into a pan. "Socks, Henry. Now. You're eight years old, for pity's sake. By your age, I was mending sheep fences in the Outback."

None of my children have seen the Outback, and neither have I. Most of my brood hasn't been past Wisconsin. Doesn't matter. I need them to believe I am invincible and all-knowing.

In the living room, cheerful voices emerge from the telly. Ah, yes, my favorite children's programs are on. Amelia is already there on the sofa. She's rarely anywhere else before noon. Wrapped in a blanket, she doomscrolls through her phone with one hand while the other is wrapped around a mug she's definitely not supposed to have.

"Amelia!" I holler. "Is that coffee you're drinking?"

She pulls the mug tighter. "It's milk with a splash of coffee. I'm hydrating."

"Hydrating *is* water, love. Not caffeine."

She snorts. "Hydrating is a state of mind."

"No coffee, Amelia. And please put on your school clothes."

Joshua slouches in the armchair, all elbows and attitude, a hoodie pulled over half of his face. He grabs the milk, chugs from the carton, and ignores the glass two inches from his hand.

"Josh, c'mon, mate," I groan. "Let's not behave like barbarians."

He shrugs, with no apologies, and sets the carton down with a thunk. "Grandma says you're supposed to use a glass, but she's not here."

"Grandma" is Florence Murgatroyd, my mother, the one-woman Queen's Guard of domestic order. She and Dad are on vacation—their first in years—leaving me alone to parent my brood for a full week. It's been a test I did not sign up for, but one I intend to survive. Fortunately, my mother-in-law, Patricia, checks in every day. Never know, I might have legged it back to England in the middle of the night.

The eggs are ready at last. I scoop them onto plates, tossing two slices of toast onto each, and herd the kids into chairs at the bar. Amelia doesn't move, but the others stampede. Henry still has no socks, but I'll deal with that once everyone has eaten.

I slide plates across the table. "Eat. Fast. The bus comes in fifteen minutes."

Charlotte takes her plate and resumes dribbling the soccer ball under the table. Josh, for a second, looks like he might say the dreaded words "thank you," then decides against it. He devours half his breakfast in a single bite.

Henry pokes his eggs. "Are these free-range?"

"They're free." I lean toward my son. "Eat them, or you'll be foraging for acorns at recess."

He snickers, then shovels in a forkful. "Did you ever have to eat acorns, Dad?"

"Don't speak while eating."

My son gives me his favorite expression—an eye roll plus a long-suffering sigh. "Well, did you eat acorns?"

"Once. I was lost in the Tasmanian bush for a week. Survived on possum jerky and eucalyptus bark."

Charlotte's eyes get big. "You're making that up."

"Does it matter if I am?" Tall tales keep me grounded, oddly, and the children love them.

The morning rolls on. After breakfast, I order Henry to find a pair of shoes—and put them on. He drops to his knees behind the bar and emerges again with a pair of well-worn sneakers. They're semi-flattened and apparently were wedged under the radiator. Oh yes, they're also crusted with a mystery substance. I wipe it off off the best I can. Then I return to the kitchen to find Charlotte and Joshua arguing over who gets the last clean fork, while Amelia barely notices the mayhem.

By the time everyone's fed, dressed, and mostly tooth-brushed, the kitchen looks like a scene from a natural disaster documentary. I step over backpacks, check the clock, and realize the bus is early.

I freeze for a split second. Then: "Shoes! Backpacks! Let's go, let's go, people!"

As I move the herd toward the front door, Henry trips over his own feet but recovers. Charlotte tries to sneak her soccer ball into her backpack. I intercept it, and my daughter seems slightly impressed. "It's not regulation size, pet. Leave it here."

She glares at me for two to three seconds, by my count, then abandons the ball on the stairs as she sprints for the door.

Amelia drags behind. "The bus isn't even here yet."

"Yeah, it is," Josh says, peeking through the curtains. "It's right outside. And the driver looks angry."

The four of them tumble out, colliding into the early morning mist like a time-lapse video of child chaos. I step onto the stoop, mug in hand, and watch as they clamber aboard. Backpacks bounce, and hair flounces. Voices are already raised in a new argument about whose backpack is the most embarrassing.

Finally, the bus drives away.

After seventy-two minutes of chatter and clacking silverware, I have peace and quiet at last.

I blow out a breath, close my eyes, and let the breeze carry the faint, sweet aroma of burnt toast and jam. When I open my eyes, the bus is a shrinking speck at the end of the street. I savor this moment, halfway between emptiness and relief.

Then, I trudge back inside. The kitchen is still a mess, but for a glorious six minutes I simply slouch on the sofa. After that, I pour another coffee—a proper cuppa this time—and enjoy the delicious aroma, not to mention the sweet silence. The chair on my left is empty. It always is these days. There's still a groove in the seat beside mine. I swear the faint trace of citrus shampoo wafts around me, as if Claudia might walk in any second and start lecturing me about cholesterol. I stare into space, remembering mornings when we'd sat here together, negotiating breakfast treaties and trading knowing looks over the kids' heads. Back when it was us against the world.

Now it's just me. Fletcher and the Four Children of the Apocalypse.

At least Claudia sends cards and small gifts to the children for birthdays and holidays. She always chooses Australian-style gifts. The kids like what she sends them, but my ex-wife has become more of a distant relative to the four beautiful youngsters she left behind.

The coffee tastes like heaven, though it's average at best. I drink slowly, watching the light creep across the kitchen tiles, turning the mess into something almost beautiful.

At precisely 8:12 a.m., I gather my coat and keys. Then I take a last look at the kitchen—the sock on the table, the puddle of juice by the fridge, the soccer ball waiting on the stairs—and I lock the door behind me. Outside, the world is cold and quiet. I pull my coat tighter and wonder if Claudia ever misses this mess, or if she's grateful to have gotten away from all of us.

She didn't just run away from me. She left the kids too—for an Australian yoga instructor.

On Millbrook Valley Road, the sun is just starting to carve the frost from the lawns. The school bus is a memory, but the exhaust remains visible. I shuffle down the path in my wrinkled shirt and tie, dodging the puddle under the mailbox.

The street is too quiet after the blast radius of my kitchen. The weight of responsibility bears down on me like a heavy blanket. I like it and hate it in equal measure. But I would never give up my children for any reason. They are my North Star, the glittering white light in my sky.

The car starts up on the second try. A minor victory.

I'm backing down the drive when my phone buzzes. It's a text message from the desk clerk on duty at the hotel this morning.

Emergency. Need you here ASAP. New guest. High priority.

And so, my day begins.

Chapter Two

Jennifer

I'm five minutes early. In my experience, that's four minutes too late for a job interview. The nanny agency's waiting room smells like microwaved coffee and shoe polish, which is about right for a Tuesday morning in Millbrook Valley. I had never heard of this town until eight days ago. The lady from the nanny agency had assured me this is a beautiful small town, and I'll love it.

I pick at the edge of my manila folder, tap-tap-tapping the corner against my knee. My heels drum out what sounds like Morse code against the linoleum. If it spells SOS, I'm not sure anyone would notice.

My former family—the Johnsons—pulled up stakes two months ago and moved to Manhattan for a "can't-miss opportunity." I don't blame them. Their oldest daughter, Mallory, wrote me two postcards from the Upper West Side before she completely forgot who I am. Even her cursive looked more sophisticated after a week. Mrs. Johnson offered to pay for my relocation if I wanted to stay with them. I politely told them I'm not interested in a world with more rats than trees.

Small towns fit me better. Here, I'm sure people say good morning and genuinely mean it. In the city, I'd probably wind up as a cautionary tale, one of those nannies who snaps and locks herself in the wine closet with a spiral-bound planner and a box of Wheat Thins.

The chair beneath me is vinyl and navy blue without a single crack. Every time I shift my weight, it sounds like a balloon deflating. I stare at the coffee table, which is crowded with parenting pamphlets that look like they've been thumbed through by a hundred anxious hands. Some promote "nurturing emotional intelligence"; others offer dire warnings about screen time and gluten. I try to guess how long each pamphlet has sat here by the depth of its coffee ring. The record-holder, *Your First Baby: A Survival Guide*, is practically laminated with stains.

As I glance around at the other applicants, I count three of us. There's a woman with steel-gray hair and orthopedic shoes, and a college student in a sequined headband who's spent the last seven minutes uploading selfies with her tongue sticking out. The agency receptionist, a woman who looks like she could have been a sitcom mom in the '80s, sits at her post, flipping through paperwork like she's shuffling a deck of tarot cards.

I wonder how she'd read my future. Is today the day I meet my "forever family?" Or will I be making PB&Js for an emotionally stunted software developer with joint custody? The odds are fifty-fifty. My folder holds all the usual stuff: CPR certification, background check, a few limp reference letters from families that have moved on to bigger, better nannies.

The clock on the wall clicks over to 9:00 exactly. Right on cue, the receptionist stands and clears her throat. "Jennifer Cordell?"

I rise and smooth my skirt, trying not to look like I've just spent ten minutes studying the merits of a gluten-free childhood. My shoes squeak on the floor—a last little protest from the linoleum. The other two applicants glance up, their expressions a mix of envy and relief. Finding a nanny can be a competitive business. No one wants to be here any longer than necessary.

"Right this way," the receptionist says, already turning her back.

I follow, passing a row of posters that are mostly stock images of babies wearing silly outfits. As I walk into the boxy space of the interview room, I'm bathed in fluorescent lighting. A faint whiff of disinfectant wafts around me. I have my choice of two chairs as well as a faux-wood desk and a computer that still holds a floppy disk. The wall calendar is stuck on February, but the dry-erase board beckons me with "Welcome, New Families!" in green bubble letters.

The woman behind the desk is not what I expected. She's younger than I expected—late thirties, maybe, with sharp features and a chic haircut that must've cost at least a hundred dollars. Her suit is almost dayglow pink, which seems inappropriate for the Midwest. Or anywhere except a gaudy big city.

"Jennifer!" the woman practically shouts, rising to shake my hand with almost manic fervor. "I'm Dana Wells. Thanks for coming in."

I take the seat she gestures toward. "Thanks for the opportunity. Honestly, I never imagined I might wind up in Nebraska. But I love what I've seen of Millbrook Valley so far."

Dana opens a folder—the agency copy of my application, no doubt—and runs a finger down the page. "You're an Arkansas girl?"

"Born and raised."

"Most of our candidates are transplants, or…well, passing through." She tilts her head. "What brought you here?"

That's the question I always dread. My mind jumps to the usual answers: a change of pace, a desire for a simpler life. Instead, I go with the line I'd practiced in the car. "I like knowing my neighbors, the way I did back in Hot Springs. Plus, I enjoy walking to the bakery and having them remember my order."

Dana grins and laughs. "A woman after my own heart."

She spends the next ten minutes running through basics—experience, certifications, whether I'm allergic to cats or gluten, and do I enjoy watching sports. I give all the right answers because I've done this dance before.

Then she hits me with The Question. "I have to ask, because it's not in your file. Why didn't you go to New York with your last family?"

I shrug. "Too much noise, and people rarely look you in the eye. I don't think I'm at my best when I'm somewhere I'd rather not be."

She sits there without moving or speaking for a moment, and I can see her respect for honesty warring with her suspicion that I might be too attached to small-town life.

"Fair enough," she finally says. "Would you be willing to consider positions outside Millbrook Valley?"

I shrug. "Depends on how far away it might be."

Dana grins. "Don't worry, no one's sending you to Seattle. Most of our placements remain right here in the Valley." She closes the folder. "You're a strong candidate, Jennifer. I have a few families in mind that might be a good fit."

I rise from my chair, still holding my neutral expression. But inside, a flicker of hope ignites. Or maybe it's the caffeine kicking in.

"One more thing," Dana says. "Are you open to…unusual arrangements?"

I pause, my hand clutching my folder. "Define unusual."

She leans in, almost whispering. "There's a family looking for a nanny who's…a bit more involved. Not just for the kids, but to help the whole household run. It's a bigger commitment than most nannies would want."

Something about her description of the situation makes me think of cults or reality shows. Or maybe just families who have lost their last three nannies to nervous breakdowns.

"I'm open to hearing more," I confirm, because I need a job and can't afford to be picky.

Dana smiles again. "I thought you might be."

"Um, do I have the job?"

"Not quite. First, a few explanations are in order." She sets her fingertips on the desk, leaning forward slightly. "This is a single-father situation. His ex-wife abandoned the family several years ago, which left Dad with four kids between the ages of eight and fifteen. They're a wonderful family…with issues."

I swallow hard, my throat suddenly tight. "Um, I see."

Dana comes around to my side of the desk and squeezes my shoulder lightly. "Think about it, Jennifer. Then let me know by Wednesday."

"I'll do that."

When I move to leave, Dana stops me again. "I think you could be the perfect nanny for this family. But don't let me talk you into it. Decide for yourself."

"Got it."

On my way out, I stop at the coffee table, to pick up *Your First Baby*, and flip to the back cover. The text offers an outdated 800 number and a quote from Dr. Spock. I leave the book face-down, like a playing card I'm hoping won't come up again.

As I push open the glass door to the parking lot, the receptionist gives me a little wave. The air outside is temperate and clean, and for a second, I imagine I can hear the sound of a tire swing creaking somewhere in the distance. While I walk back to my rental car, I do what Dana suggested. I think hard about whether I want to join a troubled family. She wouldn't send me to a nightmare house. I'm sure of that. But I'm not so naïve that I think any family with four kids and no mother is going to be a walk in the park.

The Honda Civic I'm renting smells like vanilla air freshener. I sit behind the wheel for a moment, watching a woman in yoga pants chase a toddler across the parking lot. The kid's shrieking with laughter, arms pumping like he's training for the Olympics.

Four kids. Ages eight to fifteen.

Maybe this time I'll find my forever family. Or else I'll merely survive another season.

Either way, it beats Manhattan.

Chapter Three

Fletcher

I'm supposed to be working, but instead, I find myself staring at the front door, hoping the next stranger I let into my home isn't going to tie-dye my children or burn sage in the crawlspace. The last one left a salt circle around my mailbox and tried to convince my youngest that gnomes were real. Henry's still afraid of pointy hats.

All right, that's my latest tall tale.

If the agency brings me another hippy, I'm going to start interviewing ex-military women. There must be a middle ground between Shamanic Mary Poppins and General Patton, but apparently nobody at "Millbrook Valley Nanny Solutions" got the memo.

I pace the hallway, phone in hand, waiting for the inevitable text. On the kitchen counter is a printed schedule from the agency, with a yellow sticky note that says, "She's a real go-getter!" The words are underlined three times. All that tells me is that she's either chronically optimistic or she once ran a triathlon in the rain.

My phone vibrates. I glance down, bracing myself. "Ms. Jennifer Cordell will arrive at your home within ten minutes. Please provide her with the usual orientation packet. Thank you and have a delightful day!"

Delightful? That must be the agency's little joke.

I allow myself precisely five seconds to prepare for what might await me. Then I approach the coat closet and yank the door open. A shoe avalanche greets me—Henry's sneakers, Charlotte's muddy soccer cleats, one of Amelia's sparkly sandals, and Joshua's slippers. I shove everything back in there and slam the door shut. Then, I check the hallway mirror and try to smooth my hair. I look like a man who hasn't slept since 2018.

Sighing again, I lean against the wall and try to remember the last time I engaged in something resembling adult life. I'm thirty-seven years old. My ex-wife abandoned me and our four children years ago. That's not the sort of CV a nanny might look for in a client. Our house constantly smells of either bleach or cheese for some strange reason. I've taken the morning off from my general-manager position at the hotel strictly to ensure this nanny won't flee at cheetah speed.

Does a single father in need of childcare CV? *No, you imbecile. She needs to impress you, not the other way around.*

The doorbell rings, two sharp chimes. It's precisely 9:00. I blink, surprised by the punctuality, then march to the entryway. I take a breath, square my shoulders. Then I open the door.

And freeze. This charming woman is no crone. She's not a hippie either. She is…Well, not what I expected. She stands about six inches below my eye line, wearing a tidy skirt and a navy blue sweater that I imagine has survived at least two previous families. Her auburn hair is pulled into a ponytail, but a few strands have gone rogue, framing her face. She gazes up at me with the sort of polite determination usually reserved for flight attendants or social workers.

I freeze. She looks young. Might she have lied about her age to get this job? Or perhaps I'm simply old in comparison. Her green eyes draw me in, and I suddenly realize I'm blocking the doorway.

The beautiful woman gazes at me with confusion in her yes. "Mr. Fletcher?"

"Uh…yes?" I clear my throat and attempt a casual smile. "Hello, I—I'm Fletcher Murgatroyd."

She smiles, extending her hand, and for some reason I shake it. She has a solid, businesslike grip. "I'm Jennifer Cordell. The agency sent me to you. I hope it's all right that I'm a few minutes early."

I blink several times. "That's fine. The children are at school."

"Yes, I figured they would be." She peers past me, craning her neck. "Maybe we should sit on the sofa to discuss things."

"All right."

I step aside to let her in, and she moves past me with a confident stride that suggests she's used to dealing with panicky parents. Jennifer swings her gaze to the hallway and the scuff marks on the walls, the backpacks hanging from hooks, the faint aroma of this morning's burnt toast still lingering in the air.

"You have a lovely home," she says.

I can't tell whether she's being polite or if she genuinely means it. I lead Jennifer into the living room, gesturing to the sofa. She sits on the edge, back straight, hands folded on her lap the picture of professionalism. I take the armchair across from her and immediately regret it when I realize how far apart we are. Am I conducting a job interview? I suppose I am.

"So," I begin, but then stop. How can I explain my lifestyle to her? Welcome to my circus? Please don't run away screaming?

"I read through your file," Jennifer announces, breaking the silence. "Four children, ages eight to fifteen. That's quite a handful."

"That's one way to put it." I smile weakly. "The agency probably told you I'm desperate."

She tilts her head a touch. "They said you've had some turnover."

I can't stop the bitter laugh that spills out of me. "Six nannies in eighteen months. Not my proudest statistic. It's been seven weeks since the last nanny ran away while screaming about demons and satanic rites."

Jennifer doesn't seem shocked by my miniature tall tale. Instead, she lifts her brows and asks, "Was that story a joke?"

"Sort of. I like to tell my children tall tales about things like rabbits as tall as skyscrapers as a way of directing their thoughts away from the fact their mother abandoned them. But it's true that all the other nannies resigned within two days of meeting my children."

Instead, she nods thoughtfully.

"Children can sense when adults aren't committed for the long haul, and they'll act out in anxiety. They need stability."

"Is that your professional assessment?" I ask, not meaning to sound sarcastic, but I'm tired and my mental filter has worn thin. "I don't want to put my children through another round of disappointment when you give up on us."

"What I said was just an observation, not a condemnation." She opens a small notebook and wields a shiny black ballpoint pen. "Tell me about your children."

I lean back in my chair. "Where to start? Joshua's thirteen, going on thirty. He thinks he's the man of the house now. Actually, he's quite helpful. But he carries a weight on his shoulders that no child should have to bear." I pause, watching her scribble notes. "Charlotte's eleven and brilliant—too brilliant for her own good sometimes. She reads everything, questions everything, and has strong opinions about Brussels sprouts."

Jennifer's pen stops moving. "The patriarchy?"

"Last week she informed me that doing her own laundry was perpetuating gender stereotypes." I run a hand through my hair. "I told her she could test her theory by washing Joshua's clothes for him. She huffed and announced she would wear the same jeans every day until I gave in to her demands. It's a cleanliness strike, apparently. But it only lasted for two days, then she needed to change into her soccer uniform."

"Kids go through phases of all kinds." A smile tugs at the corner of Jennifer's mouth. "And the other two kids?"

"Amelia's fifteen and has an obsession with mermaids and other mythical creatures. She's also been taking baths for two hours at a time."

Jennifer's lips twitch with amusement, and her eyes sparkle in the loveliest way. Her pink lips are full and seem to beg for a kiss.

Bloody hell, man, stop fantasizing about the potential nanny.

I fuss with my shirt collar, which probably makes me seem dodgy. "The last one is Henry, who's the baby of the family at eight years old. Henry has a huge imagination, believes anything his siblings tell him, and he's obsessed with building forts out of every clean sheet in the house. I found him sleeping under the dining room table last week. Oh, and he loves his electric scooter."

Jennifer bows her head as her pen scratches across her notebook. I can't tell whether she's recording my parental failures or simply taking notes.

"That sounds like a normal eight-year-old to me," she says. Oddly, her voice has a gentle lilt that makes me think of warm apple pie. "Children seek security in different ways."

I rub my face, abruptly aware that I haven't shaved properly in two days. "Look, Ms. Cordell—"

"Jennifer, please."

"All right, Jennifer," I correct myself. "I'm not sure what the agency told you, but I need someone who's not going to leg it after three weeks. The kids deserve consistency." I lean forward, elbows on my knees. "Please be honest with me. Can you handle this family's chaos? Because that's what we are. Pure, unfiltered chaos with occasional moments of joy."

Jennifer closes her notebook and looks me straight in the eye. "Mr. Murgat—um, Murdatiroy?"

"MUR-guh-TROYD. I know it's a mouthful. Sorry."

"Never mind, I get it now." She lifts her chin, staring straight into my eyes. "Mr. Murgatroyd, I've handled everything from triplets with colic to a five-year-old who thought she was possessed by her grandmother's spirit. I don't scare easily."

"That's what all the nannies tell me." I can't hide the skepticism that creeps into my voice. "Then Charlotte conducts her science experiments in the bathtub, or Joshua builds a catapult in the garage, and suddenly they're updating their résumés." I manage a tight smile. "By the way, I'm impressed with how well you managed my surname."

She smiles, and something warm unfurls in my chest. Probably heartburn.

"You can just call me Fletcher," I say, finding myself oddly charmed by her attempt to wrap her tongue around my surname. "And I appreciate your confidence, but I don't think you understand what you're getting into with my brood. I have two sets of grandparents in the mix too—my parents and my former in-laws."

I study her expression, searching for signs of weakness or hesitation. She meets my gaze steadily, and I'm briefly distracted by the flecks of gold in her green eyes.

"The agency says you're looking for a live-in position," I say, forcing myself back to business. "Our last nanny lived in the attic room that my ex-wife had done up years ago. It's small but private."

"That sounds perfect."

"Before you agree to anything, I should warn you about our schedule. It's...unpredictable. I work at the Millbrook Grand, which is a boutique hotel. I'm the general manager and sometimes need to rush back to the hotel after hours due to minor emergencies—or a not-so-minor ones."

"I can handle all of it, Fletcher, believe me. But you'll need to trust me one hundred percent if this arrangement is going to work." She lifts her brows, staring directly into my eyes again. "The question is, should I walk out the door? Or do you intend to hire me?"

It's do-or-die time. So, I rise and bend over slightly to offer my hand. "We have a deal, Jennifer. Welcome to the Murgatroyd household."

And I pray I've made the right decision.

Chapter Four

Jennifer

I follow Fletcher up the narrow staircase, my hand trailing along the banister as we climb up to the attic. The steps creak slightly beneath our weight, announcing our presence to the empty house. I count seventeen steps before we reach a small landing with a white door. Fletcher pauses, fumbling with a set of keys, and I hold my breath without really knowing why. Something about being here alone with a man who has four kids feels almost immoral.

"It's a bit small," he warns, jingling the key in the lock. "My ex-wife decorated it years ago for her mother's visits. But after Claudia left, my mother-in-law, Patricia Sullivan, redecorated with the help of my mother, Florence Murgatroyd. They've been friends ever since."

The door swings open, and Fletcher graciously steps aside to let me enter first. I cross the threshold into what looks like a different house entirely. Sunlight streams through a large dormer window, bathing the room in warm golden light. The space isn't huge, but it's been thoughtfully arranged to maximize comfort.

"This is charming," I tell him, genuinely surprised by the feminine atmosphere.

A twin bed with a white iron frame sits against one wall, topped with a soft lavender-and-mint quilt. Beside it, a small nightstand holds a faux stained-glass lamp. The furniture is dainty—feminine in a way that doesn't match the chaos I've glimpsed downstairs. A writing desk faces the window, its surface clean despite the signs of age.

"Claudia—my ex—went through a shabby-chic phase," Fletcher explains, sounding slightly embarrassed. "I've meant to update it, but…"

"No, it's perfect," I assure him, running my fingers over the smooth surface of the dresser. "I love it."

A rectangular rug in pastel colors covers the hardwood floor. I tiptoe across it to peer into a tiny en-suite bathroom.

"Full bath," Fletcher says from behind me. "Shower only, I'm afraid. The plumbing up here is a bit temperamental."

The bathroom is clean and simple—white tiles, pedestal sink, and a shower stall just large enough that it's not cramped. A small shell-shaped dish holds a fresh bar of soap. Someone has prepared for my arrival, and the thought makes me smile. "I won't be taking two-hour mermaid baths like Amelia. This is more than adequate for my needs."

Fletcher's chuckle is short but genuine. "Thank God for that. Our water heater can't handle another sea creature in the house."

I move to the window and gaze out at the backyard. It's larger than I expected, with a swing set that's clearly seen better days but is still safe to use. A basketball hoop is mounted on a patch of concrete, and there's an above-ground pool that's currently covered.

"The pool's not huge," Fletcher confirms, coming to stand beside me. "But it fits all of us, and the kids love to splash around in it. We uncover the pool when the weather gets warm enough."

I can picture it already—four children splashing and shrieking with joy, Fletcher joining them on weekends. Maybe I'll even sit on the edge with my feet dangling in the cool water.

"Do you swim?" Fletcher asks.

"Like a flopping fish," I admit. "But I'm excellent at lounging poolside with a book."

His shoulder brushes mine as he leans closer to the window. "See the garden plot over there? Nobody's touched it in years. You're welcome to give it a go if you've got a green thumb."

I don't, but with Fletcher so close, I suddenly want to learn the breaststroke. "Never know, I might give it a try."

The proximity makes me acutely aware of him—the clean scent of his cologne, the way his breath fogs up on the window pane, and his eyes crinkle at the corners when he smiles. I step back, needing space to think clearly. I've never before reacted to a man this strongly.

I pull away from him, gesturing around the room. "So, this would be all mine?"

"Completely private, yes. There's even a lock on the door, though I can't promise the children won't try to pick it. Joshua went through a locksmith phase last summer." He shakes his head. "The bloody internet is a menace to all parents."

I laugh, picturing a determined thirteen-year-old with lock picks and a YouTube tutorial. "I'll take my chances."

Moving backward into the center of the room, I inspect the attic to make sure I want to live in this room. But I keep getting distracted. *Stop staring at Fletcher's lips, you moron.* Right, yes, I should do that. This attic is nothing like the sterile guest rooms I've occupied in other people's homes. This space, despite its modest size, has a feminine aura that I sense could become mine like no place in Arkansas ever had. Not even my childhood bedroom felt this right.

"It's perfect," I declare again. "Thank you for showing me this room."

Fletcher shifts his weight from one foot to the other. His nervousness is endearing. "Come this way, Jennifer. I'd like to show you the sitting area that's through the door over there. It's small, but you could use it as a private living room if you need to escape the madness downstairs."

The thought of having my own sanctuary within this chaotic household seals the deal. I can already imagine myself curled up with a book after the children are in bed, maybe with a cup of tea and the quiet satisfaction of a day well spent.

"Shall we check it out?" Fletcher asks, already heading for the door.

I trail after him, already feeling more at home in the Murgatroyd house than I ever expected I might. The sitting area is just as Fletcher described—small but cozy. A loveseat upholstered in faded blue fabric sits beneath a sloped ceiling, accompanied by a reading lamp and a side table that holds a stack of dog-eared paperbacks. The space has a lived-in ambiance, as though someone once spent many hours here, though a thin layer of dust suggests recent neglect.

Fletcher wipes a finger across the table and frowns at the dust it collects. "This little hideaway hasn't been used often. Mum and Dad bought a place nearby, but they still stay over sometimes when they watch the kids. Or they used to. Now this attic hideaway will belong to you—if you take the job."

I mentally file away all of what Fletcher has told me so far. My gaze drifts to the wall, where a collection of framed photographs hangs in a cheerful jumble. I step closer, drawn to these glimpses into the Murgatroyd family life.

"You can sit," Fletcher says, gesturing to the loveseat. "We should talk details before you commit."

What strikes me most about the family photos on the wall is how often Fletcher appears in these candid moments. Unlike many family photos where the dad is clearly behind the camera, he's right in the thick of things—covered in mud during what looks like a disastrous camping trip, wearing a tiara at what must be a tea party, laughing with chocolate cake smeared across his face.

"Your kids look very happy, Fletcher."

He sighs, the sound both proud and weary. "They are. Most of the time. But they will lead you on a merry chase if you let them. That's only been since my ex-wife left us."

I finally settle onto the seat, and Fletcher settles in beside me, leaving a respectable distance between us. The cushion dips beneath his weight, sliding me fractionally closer to him. I resist the urge to shift away, not wanting to seem uncomfortable with his proximity. I absolutely will not admit to him that I'd love to taste his lips.

He rubs the back of his hand repeatedly. "All right, for the big question…After seeing the chaos that is the Murgatroyd household, are you still interested in the position? It would be full-time, live-in, with two days off per week. We can discuss which days work best for you. The salary is…"

He names a figure that's significantly more generous than I expected. I try not to let my surprise show.

As I glance back at the photos, the joy evident in each image is captured in the moment. Behind the mischief and chaos, there's love in this family—the kind that can't be faked for a camera.

"I can see myself fitting in perfectly here," I admit, surprising myself with how true that statement sounds. "I like a good challenge. And there's plenty of joy to balance it out."

Fletcher's shoulders relax slightly. "You say that now but wait until you've experienced Amelia's mermaid phase in full swing, or one of Joshua's 'improvements' to the household appliances."

I laugh, genuinely delighted by the prospect of these quirky children.

"So, you'll, ah…take the job?" Fletcher asks, hope brightening his voice.

I nod decisively as a sense of rightness settles over me. "Yes, I will take the job."

He blows out a gusty breath, his shoulders relaxing, and gives me the sweetest little smile. "Thank heavens. The kids will be home from school at three. That gives us—" he checks his watch—"about four hours to go over schedules, house rules, emergency contacts, and all that thrilling administrative bollocks."

I grin. "Perfect. And Fletcher?"

"Yes?"

"Thank you for trusting me with your family."

He lifts an eyebrow. "Don't thank me yet. Talk to me in a month if you're still standing."

Despite his words, I sense warmth in his voice, the kind that suggests he thinks—hopes—I might be different from the others who came before me. And I'm suddenly determined to prove him right.

We both rise from our seats, bumping into each other in the process. His fingers brush against my breast accidentally, and he takes a half step backward, clearing his throat.

My cheeks grow warm, and my imagination takes an abrupt and unprofessional turn. In my mind, I see myself reaching forward, grasping his shirt with both hands, dragging him closer until my chest meets his. I picture my fingers working at his tie, loosening it with urgent tugs before I rip open his shirt, sending buttons flying across the carpet. My hands would slip beneath the waistband of those perfectly fitted slacks, finding heated skin and firm muscle.

I blink hard, trying to banish the wicked fantasy. What is wrong with me? I've been in this house less than an hour. I've barely met the man. And he's my employer, for heaven's sake.

Stop it, I scold myself. This is the best job opportunity I've had in years. Four children who need stability and care. A beautiful home. A generous salary. I can't risk all that because their father happens to fill out a pair of slacks better than any man has a right to. But I force myself to focus, to be professional. These children have suffered a parade of nannies who, quite frankly, should never work as caregivers ever again. These kids need someone dependable, someone who won't abandon them when things get tough. I could be that person. I *want* to be that person.

I *am* that person.

But as Fletcher turns to face me, running a hand through his already tousled hair, my resolve weakens.

"Are you all right?" he asks, noticing my flushed face. "Is it too hot in here? The thermostat has been temperamental since Joshua tried to 'upgrade' it."

"I'm fine," I manage, though my voice sounds strained even to my own ears.

He's standing so close now that I can smell his cologne—something woody and subtle. Close enough that I could count each of his eyelashes if I wanted. Close enough that if I leaned forward just a few inches…

Without thinking, without planning, I rise slightly on my toes and press my lips to his. The kiss is brief but electric, a spark that ignites every nerve ending in my body. His lips are warm and surprisingly soft, and for a split second, they yield to mine before I pull back abruptly. Horror floods through me as I register what I've just done. Fletcher's eyes are wide with shock, his mouth slightly open. The silence between us stretches, charged and dangerous.

"I'm—I'm sorry," I stammer, my cheeks burning so hot I'm sure they must be as red as Rudolph's nose. "That was completely inappropriate. I don't know what I was thinking."

Fletcher blinks rapidly, one hand rising to touch his lips as if confirming what just happened. "I, um…"

"Please forget I did that," I say quickly, mortification making my heart pound painfully against my ribs. "It won't happen again. I promise, I'm normally much more professional."

He clears his throat, a flush creeping up his neck. "It's, ah…it's been a long time since anyone…I mean, I wasn't expecting…"

We stand here in awkward silence, neither knowing quite what to say. The thought that I might have just wrecked the best job I've been offered in years with one impulsive, unprofessional act. What was I thinking?

The truth is, I wasn't thinking at all. And now I might have ruined everything before it's even begun.

Chapter Five

Fletcher

Jennifer kissed me. The nanny slipped her tongue between my lips and *kissed* me. She seemed horrified by what she'd done, though she paid no attention to my growing erection. The last thing I want is to become a stereotype of a single father who shags the nanny. What would the children think? What would my parents think? Or my in-laws? My stomach twists as I realize this could turn into a complete disaster.

"Jennifer," I begin, then stop. I have no bloody idea what to say.

She backs away, her eyes wide, and bites down on her bottom lip. "I'm so sorry, Fletcher. That was completely out of line. I have no idea what came over me."

As I shove a hand through my hair, I struggle to process what just happened. "It was…unexpected, for sure."

"I understand if you want to rescind the job offer."

Something about her embarrassment makes me feel protective. It's been ages since I've felt that way toward a woman who wasn't a friend or relative. "No, the job offer stands. We're both adults. We can acknowledge this was a singular moment of madness and move past it."

Jennifer blows out a breath, her shoulders flagging. "Thank you, Fletcher. I swear that won't happen again."

I struggle to ignore the way my pulse is still hammering. "No worries. Moving past it seems like the most prudent option."

But as I watch her smoothing down her skirt and straightening her shoulders, I realize that moving past it might not be as easy as it sounds. The taste of her lips lingers on mine, and I wonder what might have happened if I hadn't been quite so shocked. If I'd kissed her back instead of standing there like a bloody statue.

Christ, man. Get it together.

"Should we head to the backyard?" I suggest, needing distance from this small, intimate space. "Let me show you the aboveground pool and the treehouse, then we can go over the children's routines."

"That all sounds perfect." Jennifer's voice is steadier now, more professional. She tucks a strand of hair behind her ear, a nervous gesture that I find oddly endearing. "Let's go."

I lead the way through the kitchen and out the back door. The yard is larger than it appears from the window, with a lawn that isn't enormous but is well kept and vegetable garden that's been overtaken by weeds. I point toward the covered pool.

"We usually open it in May," I explain, grateful for the neutral topic. "The kids practically live in it during summer holidays."

"But it's June, and you haven't removed the pool cover yet."

"Ah, yes." I grimace. "My job at the hotel has taken up a large part of my summer so far. One disaster after another. That's part of why I need a nanny."

"I'd be happy to get the pool set up for you." Jennifer smiles politely, keeping a professional distance between us now. "Do the children all know how to swim?"

"Joshua and Charlotte are strong swimmers. Amelia thinks she's part mermaid. Henry's still working on his swimming lessons. He can manage a doggy paddle across the shallow end. Joshua swims well and loves to belly flop into the pool strictly to make the girls shriek."

"Sounds like a happy, loving family."

"Yes, we are that."

I watch her surveying the yard, noting that she spots the basketball hoop with its frayed net, the swing set that needs new chains, the sandbox that's become a toilet for our neighbor's cat than a play area. I haven't had time to deal with those issues. While most nannies see only maintenance problems, Jennifer clearly notes the possibilities.

"There's a treehouse," I point toward the ancient oak at the back of the property. "Joshua built it last summer with minimal adult supervision. It's structurally questionable but somehow still standing. I ordered the children to stay away from it until I can fix the problems."

Jennifer shades her eyes with her hand, squinting up at the wooden platform wedged between thick branches. "Looks like it has character."

"That's one word for it. The fire department had to retrieve Charlotte from it twice last year. She kept climbing up but forgetting she's afraid of heights."

"Classic eleven-year-old logic."

I study her profile as she examines the yard. The afternoon light catches the highlights in her hair auburn, and I notice that she unconsciously toys with her earring when she's concentrating. *Professional distance*, I remind myself. We've already crossed one forbidden line today.

"The children's schedules are fairly straightforward," I explain, pulling my phone out of my pocket. But I realize I'm not actually looking at my phone. I'm staring at Jennifer's lips again, remembering how soft they felt against mine for that brief, electric moment.

Focus, you bloody moron.

My trousers have grown tighter, though fortunately, not enough that she might have noticed. I clear my throat and focus on the screen. "Joshua has football practice on Tuesdays and Thursdays. Charlotte has soccer practice on Wednesdays. Amelia refuses to commit to any activities because she's convinced they'll interfere with her 'transformation schedule,' whatever that means."

Jennifer pulls out her own notebook again and begins scribbling. I notice her hand trembles slightly as she writes. At least I'm not the only one still rattled by what happened earlier.

"And Henry?" she asks.

"He has swimming lessons on Saturdays, though he spends most of the time trying to dupe his instructor into believing his sister Amelia is actually a mermaid who lives in the pool." I scroll through my calendar, focusing on the task at hand instead of the lingering sensation of Jennifer's lips against mine. "Henry also has a standing playdate with the neighbor's son on Saturday afternoons. They build elaborate LEGO structures and make up ridiculous stories about them."

Jennifer grins. "That sounds adorable."

Then her attention returns to her notepad, and her pen moves quickly across the page. She's all business now, as if the kiss never happened. I should be relieved.

I'm not.

Jennifer puts away her pen and notepad. "I think I've got everything I need for now. The rest I can find out on my own when the kids get home."

"I need to make an appearance at work. I should probably check in, make sure everything's running smoothly." I clear my throat, trying to sound like a responsible adult instead of a man who just kissed his new employee. "Will you be all right here on your own for a few hours?"

"Of course." She adjusts her purse strap, looking every inch the competent nanny. "I'd like to get settled in my room, maybe familiarize myself with the house layout before the children arrive. But I won't peek into their rooms. Kids need their privacy, especially with a stranger joining the family."

I nod and move toward the front door, though part of me wants to stay right here with Jennifer. To see how she'll react to Joshua's collection of dismantled electronics in the hallway closet. Or Charlotte's "Twelve Rules of Living with brothers" that she taped to her bedroom door.

"The spare key is under the ceramic frog by the front steps," I tell Jennifer. "I know it's not the most secure hiding spot, but with four children constantly losing their keys..."

"Don't worry about it. I understand completely."

I check my watch. "I really must head to the hotel. I've been away longer than planned."

"Go, go," Jennifer says, making a shooing motion with her hands. "I've got this. You'll be back before the children come home. I'm looking forward to finally meeting them."

With the front door halfway open, I turn my head to glance at Jennifer. "If the little monsters should arrive early for some reason..."

"Relax, Fletcher. I promise not to let the kids bamboozle me with tall tales about family life in the Murgatroyd clan."

"I'm impressed that you've already mastered our family's odd surname."

Jennifer's smile is warm enough to melt butter. "Well, I wouldn't want to say it wrong when I meet the children."

I linger at the door, reluctant to leave despite knowing I should. The hotel will be in chaos without me. My assistant manager, Debbie, is capable but easily flustered when the owner's wife, Iris Wheeler, makes her surprise inspections.

"One more thing," I say, my hand still on the doorknob. "The children don't know about their mother. I mean, they know she left and that she's in Australia with her Aussie yoga instructor boyfriend. But they don't know about Claudia's postpartum depression that lasted long after she gave birth to Henry. I think that's why she left her children behind, though that's no excuse."

"I understand. That's not my story to tell."

"Thank you."

With that, I finally force myself to walk out the door. The sun blinds me as I walk to my car, and I catch myself glancing back at the house. Through the kitchen window, I can see Jennifer moving about, already making herself at home.

The drive to The Millbrook Grand takes twelve minutes, but my mind isn't on traffic or the quarterly reports waiting on my desk. I keep replaying that kiss. The way Jennifer rose onto her tiptoes, the soft pressure of her lips, how she tasted faintly of mint and something else I can't identify. Something sweet and inviting.

I shake my head, determined to keep my eyes on the road. Thinking that way will inevitably lead to disaster. I've hired Jennifer to care for my children, not to complicate my already chaotic life with romantic entanglements. But bloody hell, when was the last time a woman kissed me? Really kissed me, not just a polite peck on the cheek from one of the school mums at a parent-teacher meeting.

My phone buzzes as I pull into the hotel car parking lot. It's a text from Debbie: *Mrs. Hartwell is here asking about the wedding preparations for next weekend. She's in your office.*

I growl under my breath. Iris Wheeler is known for her ability to find fault with everything from the thread count in the linens to the angle of the flower arrangements. Her husband, Clarence, is much more reasonable.

I count to ten and then march inside.

The Millbrook Grand isn't actually grand by London standards. But for a small American town, it's quite respectable. Victorian architecture with modern amenities, the kind of place that hosts wedding receptions and corporate retreats. I've been managing it for five years now, ever since Claudia and I moved here for what she called "a simpler life."

Ironic, considering she buggered off to Australia for an even simpler life with a man who can bend his leg behind his head.

I shove those thoughts aside and get to work.

Chapter Six

Jennifer

What does a nanny do when no one is home? I can't speak for all nannies. But me? I do the most boring things for two and half hours. I sweep the kitchen floor, wipe down the counters, and organize the spice rack that's in complete disarray. I stumble onto several jars of cinnamon, though one seems unusually empty. What happened to the rest of it? Don't think I'll plumb that mystery just yet.

Then I clean up the living room, vacuuming the carpet that's covered in what looks like glitter and Cheerios. Someone has built a fort with sofa cushions in the corner, which I carefully dismantle and reconstruct properly. It's clearly Henry's work—there's a hand-drawn sign that says, "NO GIRLS ALLOWED," that's taped to one of the pillows. I find myself smiling as I fold a pile of clean laundry that's been sitting in a basket for who knows how long. There's something soothing about bringing order to the chaos, like I'm already carving out my place in this household.

After tidying up, I unpack my meager belongings in my new attic sanctuary. Two suitcases contain my entire life—clothes neatly folded, a few cherished books, and the small wooden box my grandmother gave me before she passed away. Not much to show for twenty-eight years on this earth, but I've always traveled light.

My phone buzzes with a text from Fletcher: *Running late. Children should be home any minute. Good luck.*

Any minute?!? Holy shit! *Thanks for the head's up, boss man.*

I hadn't realized I'd been tidying up for three hours. I do fall into a Zen trance-like state whenever I clean. Still, I would've appreciated a longer lag time before the barbarians descend.

Right on cue, I hear the front-door latch click into place, followed by the thunderous noise of backpacks hitting the floor and voices talking over each other. I'm careful not to intrude too much. This isn't my home yet.

Then the door bursts open, and four children tumble inside.

"Dad?" A boy's voice, cracking slightly.

I walk toward the front hallway, my heart beating faster than it should. This is it—my first real test as the new caregiver for these kids. As I round the corner of the hallway, I call out, "Your dad's still at work, sweetie. I'm Jennifer, your new nanny. Didn't your daddy tell you?"

Four pairs of eyes gape at me from the entryway. The oldest boy—Joshua, I assume—stands protectively in front of his siblings like a miniature bodyguard. He's tall for thirteen, with Fletcher's dark hair and the kind of serious expression that makes him seem older than his years.

"Where's Dad?" he asks, suspicion coloring his voice.

"At the hotel. He'll be home soon." I keep my voice calm and friendly. "You must be Joshua."

He nods curtly, then gestures to his siblings. "Charlotte, Amelia, Henry."

Charlotte steps forward, her chin jutting out defiantly. She's wearing a T-shirt emblazoned with the logo of a soccer team, the Millbrook Valley Mustangs. The logo includes a soccer ball and, naturally, a wild mustang.

"Are you the new nanny?" she asks, eyeing me up and down like I'm a specimen under a microscope.

"Yes, I am." I smile, trying not to show how nervous I actually am. "Your dad hired me this morning. I thought he must've told you."

"Probably forgot. Dad's scatterbrained sometimes."

"I can understand that. He works very hard, doesn't he?"

When Charlotte nods, I add, "I'm here to help your dad—and all of you. How does that sound?"

Charlotte shrugs. "Sounds okay, I guess."

I smile and touch her arm gently. "I bet we'll be friends very soon."

"Did you sign a contract?" Amelia pipes up from behind her brother. She's the oldest at fifteen and has blonde hair. "The last nanny didn't sign a contract, and she only lasted two weeks."

"Yes, I did sign a contract. I'm here for the long haul."

The youngest—Henry—peeks out from behind Joshua. His eyes are so wide they seem ready to burst out of their sockets. "Are you gonna stay?"

His whisper somehow carries across the entire living room.

My heart melts a little at his question. "I'm going to try my very best to stay, Henry."

"The last nanny said that too," Amelia mutters, but there's more hurt than hostility in her voice.

I crouch down to Henry's eye level, ignoring the way my skirt bunches awkwardly. "You know what? I don't blame you for being suspicious. But I'm different from the other nannies."

"How?" Joshua crosses his arms, still playing the role of family protector.

"Well, for starters, I reorganized your spice cabinet and found some jars of cinnamon. The biggest one was almost empty. That's either a sign of extreme dedication to baking or complete chaos. I'm betting on chaos."

Joshua cocks his head to one side, considering me. "Dad says we're not allowed to have cinnamon after The Incident."

"The Incident?" I raise an eyebrow.

"Henry climbed onto a stool to get a bottle of cinnamon, but he dropped it and the cinnamon got all over his hair and even in his nose." Charlotte explains. "He sneezed it all over Dad's work laptop and got in deep doo-doo for destroying it."

I bite my lip to keep from laughing. "Well, that explains the empty cinnamon jar in the cupboard. Maybe we should stick to sugar from now on when we bake. It's easier to vacuum up."

This earns me a tiny smile from Henry, who's still partially hidden behind Joshua.

"Are you guys hungry?" I ask, glancing at the clock. "I could make a snack while we wait for your dad."

"We always have cookies after school," Henry pipes up, suddenly more animated.

Amelia sighs dramatically. "Henry, we don't *always* have cookies. Dad says too much sugar makes you bounce off the walls."

"But I bounce really good," Henry argues, demonstrating with a little hop that nearly knocks over an umbrella stand.

I catch it just in time, steadying both the stand and Henry with one practiced move. "Careful there, buddy. How about we compromise? Cookies today to celebrate my first day, and something healthier tomorrow?"

Joshua narrows his eyes. "You're trying to bribe us."

"Absolutely," I admit with a grin. "Is it working?"

A reluctant smile tugs at his lips. "Maybe."

I lead the parade of suspicious children into the kitchen, where I'd already spotted a package of chocolate chip cookies in the pantry. As I arrange them on a plate, four pairs of eyes study my every move.

"Where are these cookies from?" Charlotte asks, peering at the package like she's conducting a forensic investigation.

"Your pantry," I assure her. "Found them while I was cleaning up."

"Dad doesn't usually let us have the good cookies," she continues, still suspicious but accepting the treat from me.

"Well, today's special." I pour four glasses of milk, noting how they all watch me move around their kitchen. "Tell me about school. How was your day?"

Henry immediately launches into an animated story about how his teacher, Mrs. Patterson, brought her pet hamster to class and it escaped, causing what he describes as "total hamster mayhem." He waves his hands dramatically as he explains, "You'll love this! I'm re-enacting the great hamster hunt, complete with sound effects."

"You're not gonna tell us to use our 'indoor voices,' are you?" Charlotte asks, watching me intently.

"Nope. I'm more concerned with the hamster's safety than noise levels." I wink at Henry who grins back, cookie crumbs dotting his chin.

Amelia picks at her cookie, breaking it into tiny pieces. "So, how long are you actually planning to stay?"

Her tone suggests she doesn't believe I'll stick around for more than a day and a half.

I meet her gaze directly. "Until you guys are sick of me or your dad fires me. Whichever comes first."

"That could be tomorrow," Joshua warns, but I notice he's on his second cookie.

"Could be," I agree. "But I hope not. I just got unpacked, and it would be a real pain packing everything up again."

Henry tugs at my sleeve, his eyes wide. "Did you know I can burp the alphabet? Wanna hear?"

"Henry!" Charlotte groans. "That's disgusting."

"I'd actually be impressed," I say, trying not to laugh at Charlotte's horrified expression. "But maybe save that particular talent for outside, okay Henry?"

He beams at me like I've just handed him the keys to a candy store. "You're not like the other nannies."

"I'll take that as a compliment." I wipe a milk mustache from his upper lip with my thumb. The gesture seems natural, like I've been doing it for years instead of minutes.

Joshua watches this interaction with narrowed eyes. "The last nanny cried when Henry showed his pet worms to her."

"Worms don't scare me," I assure him, though I'm not exactly eager to meet Henry's slimy friends. "I grew up on a farm in Arkansas. I've seen plenty worse than worms."

That seems to impress the boys, especially Joshua. "A farm girl, huh? That's cool."

"Tell me more about these pet worms," I say to Henry, whose face lights up as if I've just offered him a lifetime supply of ice cream.

"They live in my special dirt box! I named them all after superheroes. The fattest one is Hulk." He bounces on his toes. "Wanna see them?"

The front door opens, and all the banter goes quiet.

I swivel my head around to see Fletcher shutting the door. He seems harried, as if his employees caused him trouble today. I smile brightly at him. "Welcome home, Fletcher. The kids and I were just having a little snack. Want a cookie?"

I hold one out toward him, but he shakes his head.

Henry rushes up to his father, offering him a one-third eaten cookie. "They're soooo good, Dad!"

Fletcher looks exhausted, his tie slightly askew and his hair more disheveled than when he left. But when Henry beams up at him with that chocolate-smudged grin, his entire expression softens.

"Thank you, mate," he says, accepting the mangled cookie and taking a small bite. "Mmm, delicious."

Henry giggles and bounces back to his seat. I notice the way Fletcher's eyes sweep the kitchen, taking in the clean counters and organized space. His gaze lingers on me for just a moment longer than necessary, and heat rushes through me.

"How did it go, Jennifer?" he asks, loosening his tie and then removing it completely.

"Great. We've just been getting to know each other." When he rolls up his sleeves, exposing muscular biceps, I swear my mouth waters. "We've covered hamster escapes, pet worms, and the great cinnamon disaster."

Fletcher rubs his neck. "Could you mind the children while I have a shower?"

"Of course. That's what I'm here for."

Chapter Seven

Fletcher

Jennifer smiles at me sweetly. "Take a nice long shower, Fletcher. The children and I could use more time together to get to know each other better. I'd love to learn all about their likes and dislikes, what they do in school, all that important stuff."

"That's very thoughtful of you, Jennifer."

"All part of my job."

My brows lift. "None of the previous nannies or babysitters would do anything of the sort."

She shrugs. "I believe in building relationships so I can understand what children need. They'll feel more secure when they're heard and understood." Jennifer smiles. "Besides, I'm genuinely curious about them. They seem like wonderful kids."

Her directness catches me off guard. Most nannies say what they think parents want to hear, not what they actually believe. I stare at Jennifer for a moment too long, admiring how she stands her ground with quiet confidence. "That's refreshing, Jennifer. Thank you."

"Now please, go, take your shower." She all but shoves me away while smiling sweetly. "We'll be fine down here."

I nod and trudge upstairs, my mind still replaying that impulsive kiss from earlier. The memory of it follows me into the bathroom as

I strip off my work clothes and step under the hot spray. The water pressure is pathetic—another thing on my endless list of projects—but the spray still feels heavenly against my tired muscles.

What am I doing? I've hired a nanny who kissed me within hours of meeting me, and instead of being appalled, I can't stop thinking about it. *About her.* Those full breasts. The way she licks her lips whenever she glances at me. Oh, and I can't forget her sexy legs. I begin to imagine myself hovering over her on all fours, admiring her naked body. And then I plunge my cock deep inside her luscious body.

Bloody hell. I should not fantasize about the nanny.

While I scrub shampoo through my hair with more force than necessary, I experience a flash of insight. Fantasizing about the nanny will only ever lead to disaster. Four children, a demanding job, and now a beautiful nanny who tastes like mint and reminds me of things I'd forgotten I could feel. The rational part of my brain insists I should maintain professional boundaries. But the other part—the side that's been dormant for too long—keeps replaying the moment when her warm lips yielded to mine.

I rinse the soap from my hair and reach for the body wash. As I lather it across my chest, my treacherous mind conjures images of Jennifer's hands replacing mine. Her fingers trailing down my torso, and lower, wrapping around—

What is wrong with me? I'm getting hard just thinking about the nanny.

Faint pounding originates from somewhere downstairs. As I cup my cock with one hand, I realize the racket seems to be getting louder—and closer.

"No, Henry!" a feminine voice calls out. "Your daddy is—"

The bathroom door flies open, revealing my half-naked, half-aroused self to an eight-year-old boy. *Oh, bollocks.* Luckily, the frosted shower door hides my erection. Quite frankly, my hard-on deflated the moment the bathroom door flew open.

"Dad!" Henry shouts as he yanks the shower door open, completely oblivious to my state of undress as I frantically grab a towel to cover myself. "Jennifer said I could show you my new drawing, but she also said I should wait. But I really really wanted to show you now because it's a dinosaur eating our neighbor's cat and—"

"Henry!" Jennifer appears behind him, slightly out of breath, her cheeks pink from exertion. "I told you your father was showering!"

She lifts her brows as she notices my wet, towel-covered lower body. A blush fires up on her cheeks, and for a moment, we're both frozen in an awkward tableau—me clutching a towel around my waist, Jennifer standing in my bathroom doorway looking mortified, and Henry bouncing between us with a crumpled piece of paper.

"Out," I command, jabbing a finger toward the door while keeping one hand firmly on my towel. "Both of you. *Now.*"

Henry's face falls. "But Daddy, my dinosaur—"

"Show me when I'm dressed." I struggle to keep my voice gentle. "Give me two minutes, all right?"

Jennifer mouths to me, "I'm sorry." Then she grabs Henry's shoulders, steering him toward the door. "Come on, sweetheart. Your daddy needs privacy."

But as she turns to leave, her gaze drops briefly to my chest, lingering on the water droplets trailing down my torso. Her lips part slightly, and I watch her throat work as she swallows hard. The moment stretches out between us, charged with the same electricity from our kiss earlier. Even with Henry chattering beside her, even in this ridiculous situation, I experience that same pull as if a large magnet draws us together.

Then she blinks, clearly embarrassed, and rushes Henry out of the bathroom. The door closes with a soft click, leaving me alone with my racing thoughts and cooling water.

I finish my shower quickly, scrubbing away the remnants of my workday along with my inappropriate thoughts about the new nanny—my employee. When I step out of the shower stall, I wrap the towel securely around my waist and peer at my reflection in the mirror. I look exhausted. It's the sort of weariness that comes from years of solo parenting and never-ending responsibilities.

"Pull yourself together," I mutter to my reflection. "She's the nanny, not a potential girlfriend."

After dressing in jeans and a clean t-shirt, I head downstairs to find Jennifer sitting cross-legged on the living room floor with

Henry, admiring his dinosaur artwork. Charlotte is nearby, actually reading a book instead of explaining her favorite soccer moves. Joshua is nowhere to be seen, probably tinkering with something mechanical in the room he shares with Henry. Amelia has transformed the dining room table into an art studio, surrounded by colored pencils and what looks like a half-finished drawing of a mermaid.

"Dad!" Henry jumps up when he spots me, waving his dinosaur picture frantically. "Look! It's a T-Rex eating Mrs. Pinkerton's cat because it keeps pooping in our sandbox!"

I crouch to examine the surprisingly detailed drawing. "That's quite creative, Henry. Though perhaps we shouldn't show this particular masterpiece to Mrs. Pinkerton."

"But her cat is a sandbox pooper," Henry insists, deadly serious. "Somebody should tell her."

Jennifer stifles a laugh, her eyes meeting mine over Henry's head. "I suggested maybe the dinosaur could scare the cat away instead of eating it, but Henry feels strongly about artistic integrity."

"Naturally," I agree. "Eight-year-olds are very serious about drawings of dinosaurs."

Jennifer grins at me, and the way the afternoon light streams through the window catches the gold flecks in her green eyes. "He's quite passionate about his art."

"I can see that." I ruffle Henry's hair, trying to ignore how domestic this scene seems—me coming home to find Jennifer seamlessly integrated into my family's chaos. "Why don't you show Jennifer your other drawings while I check on Joshua and the girls?"

Henry nods eagerly and scampers off to retrieve his art collection. As he disappears upstairs, Jennifer rises gracefully from the floor, smoothing down her skirt.

"How was work?" she asks, her voice carrying that same warm tone that made me hire her this morning. Was it only this morning? Feels like a lifetime ago.

"Typical hotel crisis management," I inform her. "Mrs. Hartwell found fault with everything from the tablecloth angles to the temperature of the reception hall." I rake my fingers through my still-damp hair. "But enough about my day. How did things really go here?"

Jennifer smiles sweetly, genuinely, with no trace of the polite mask most nannies wear. "They're wonderful children, Fletcher. Henry showed me his worm collection—all named after superheroes. Charlotte explained why the HAARP arrays in Alaska are responsible for her inability to wash the dishes properly. And Amelia gave me a detailed lecture on mermaid biology."

"Sounds about right." I lean against the doorframe, studying her face while she talks. I sense genuine affection in her voice when she mentions my children. "What about Joshua?"

"Ah, Joshua." Her expression grows thoughtful. "He's protective. Suspicious. Asked me three times if I'm really planning to stay." Jennifer pauses. "I can see why. He's carrying a lot of responsibility for someone his age."

Her observation hits me square in the chest. But I can't think about that right now. I want to see what children have been up to while I was in the shower. When the house is too quiet, I start to worry. Having clever children can be a blessing and a curse, but I would never want them to change.

I walk into the hall, waving for Jennifer to follow me. The house is quiet now. Too quiet. I've been a father long enough to know that silence usually means trouble.

"Joshua?" I call out, heading toward the stairs. "What are you up to, mate?"

No answer. My parental radar starts pinging.

Jennifer follows close behind me, both our footsteps light on the hardwood floor. I try my best to avoid focusing on her lush hips rather than the curve of her lips or the way her skirt hugs her hips.

"Is this normal?" she whispers. "The silence?"

"About as normal as a peaceful night at the zoo." I shout again, louder this time. "Joshua!"

Finally, his voice drifts down from upstairs. "In my room, Dad!"

I take the stairs two at a time with Jennifer right behind me. I hesitate at Joshua's door, which is slightly ajar. A strange mechanical whirring sound comes from inside, along with the unmistakable smell of burning plastic.

"Joshua?" I push the door open to find my thirteen-year-old son hunched over his desk, safety goggles perched on his nose, wielding what appears to be my electric toothbrush attached to… "is that my electric razor?"

"Hi, Dad!" he says cheerfully, not looking up from his contraption. "I'm making a mini-hovercraft. Almost got it working."

What the bloody hell has Josh done this time?

Chapter Eight

Jennifer

I suspect Fletcher's oldest son has taken advantage of his brief absence to plot something big. The smell of burning plastic is getting stronger, and Joshua's "mini-hovercraft" looks suspiciously like it contains parts from several expensive household appliances.

"Joshua Stephen Murgatroyd, I asked you a question." Fletcher spoke those words in his sternest dad voice. It makes even my spine straighten. "Is that my electric razor?"

"Um, yeah." Josh's shoulders hunch defensively. "I needed the motor. The toothbrush one wasn't powerful enough."

I struggle to keep from laughing, which results in soft snorts. This is exactly the kind of childhood ingenuity that would've gotten me grounded for a month back in Arkansas.

Fletcher pinches the bridge of his nose, shutting his eyes briefly. "And where's the rest of my razor?"

"In the…garbage can out back?" Joshua offers hopefully.

I step forward, hoping to defuse the situation. "That's quite the engineering project you've got there. Maybe next time we could get you proper materials instead of dismantling household appliances. Would that work?"

I give Joshua my most encouraging smile.

His eyes light up. "You'd get me real parts? Like motors and stuff?"

"If your dad approves, sure." I glance at Fletcher, whose expression has softened from outrage to resignation.

"We'll discuss it later," he replies. I'm learning that's dad-code for 'maybe.' He holds out his palm. "For now, hand over what's left of my razor."

Joshua reluctantly surrenders his creation. As Fletcher examines the mangled remains of his grooming tool, I notice Amelia and Charlotte hovering in the doorway, exchanging meaningful glances.

"What are you two plotting?" I ask, turning toward them.

Charlotte spreads her arm, her expression full of practiced innocence. "Nothing."

Amelia twirls a strand of hair around her finger, trying too hard to seem casual. "We were just wondering what's for dinner."

"Uh-huh." I cross my arms and narrow my eyes. "And I'm Mary Poppins. Spill it, girls."

They exchange another look, and Charlotte sighs dramatically. "Fine. We were going to ask if we could have a sleepover tonight."

"On a school night?" Fletcher asks, still holding the mutilated razor.

"It's for a school project," Amelia says quickly. "Charlotte needs help with her science experiment about sleep patterns. Four of my friends have signed up."

I raise an eyebrow. "That sounds suspiciously well-rehearsed."

Fletcher glances at me with his lips twitching slightly as if he's about to laugh. "They've been practicing that excuse since breakfast, I'd wager."

"Dad!" Charlotte protests, but she's fighting a smile.

"How about this," I suggest, sidling between the father and his daughters before this turns into a full-on negotiation. "Why don't we start with dinner? Then we can discuss sleepovers and science projects."

"What's for dinner?" Henry's pipes up from behind us. He appeared in the doorway clutching his dinosaur drawing and what looks like a handful of actual dirt.

"Henry," Fletcher sighs, "why do you have soil in your hands?"

"I brought Hulk to meet everyone." Henry opens his palm to reveal a fat earthworm writhing in a clump of mud. "He wanted to see my room."

Amelia shrieks and jumps backward into Charlotte, who stumbles into the doorframe.

Joshua glances up from his dismantled hovercraft. "Can I use Hulk for my next experiment?"

Fletcher wipes a hand across his face, then sighs. "Let's talk about that another time. Please clean up this mess now."

While the kiddos begin picking up all the stuff they've cached here, there, and everywhere, I sidle closer to Fletcher. In a half-whisper, I tell him, "Their behavior is due to the excitement of a new person coming into their home. I'm sure that's all it was, and things will settle down soon."

"You're probably right," Fletcher murmurs back, but his eyes are focused on my lips again. We're standing so close that I can smell his soap—something masculine and woodsy that smells so delicious I'd love to lick it all off his skin.

"I should start dinner," I suggest quickly, scuffling backward before I do something stupid like kiss him again. "What do the children usually eat?"

"Whatever doesn't require too much effort," Fletcher admits with a sheepish grin. "I'm not exactly Gordon Ramsay in the kitchen."

"Don't worry, I'll make dinner." I can see the turmoil unfolding in Joshua's room. "Finish cleaning up, everyone. Dinner in thirty minutes."

As I head downstairs, I hear Fletcher corralling the children behind me, his voice a mixture of exasperation and affection. I feel as if I'm already becoming part of this tightknit, loving family.

The kitchen seems different now that I'm no longer just a visitor organizing someone else's space. I'm the one making dinner, the one creating something for this family. I gather ingredients from the fridge and pantry, mentally cataloging what I have to work with. Chicken breasts, pasta, some vegetables that have seen better days but are still salvageable. Nothing fancy, but I can whip something up quickly. I've always been good at stretching ingredients.

As I begin heating oil in a large skillet, I hear the thunderous sound of four children racing down the stairs. They burst into the kitchen like a small army, with Fletcher trailing behind and looking slightly shell-shocked.

"Wow, it smells yummy in here already," Charlotte announces, hopping onto one of the bar stools at the kitchen island.

"I haven't even started cooking yet, sweetie," I laugh as I season the chicken. "That's just the butter melting in the pan."

Charlotte grins. "Daddy usually burns the butter."

"I do not burn the butter," Fletcher protests, leaning against the counter beside me. "I occasionally...over-caramelize it."

"That's grown-up talk for burning," Henry pipes up, swinging his legs from his perch on the stool. "Grandma says so."

I wink at him. "No burning tonight. Cross my heart."

Fletcher moves closer, ostensibly to observe me cooking, but I'm acutely aware of his proximity. His arm brushes mine as he reaches for a glass from the cabinet, and I nearly drop the spatula. How can that man smell so damn good all the time? It isn't fair.

"May I help?" he asks, his voice low enough that only I can hear.

I glance up at him, noting the way his eyes seem darker in the kitchen lighting. "You could boil water for the pasta."

"I think I can manage that without causing a catastrophe." His self-deprecating smile makes me want to hug him.

But instead, I hand Fletcher a large pot, our fingers brushing as he accepts it. The brief contact sends electricity rushing through me, and I need to focus extra hard on not overcooking the chicken.

"Jennifer?" Henry's voice draws my attention. "Do you like worms?"

"They're, um...useful creatures," I say diplomatically, flipping the chicken pieces. "They help gardens grow."

"See!" Henry announces triumphantly to his siblings. "I told you she'd understand!"

Amelia rolls her eyes. "Henry, normal people don't keep worms as pets." She scrunches her nose up in disgust. "They're gross little slimy things."

"Hulk isn't gross," Henry argues. "He's special."

"Where is Hulk now?" I ask, suddenly concerned about earthworm hygiene in the family's kitchen.

"Back in his dirt box in my room," Henry assures me. "Dad made me put him back after the bathroom incident."

Fletcher shoots Henry a warning look. "We don't need to discuss the bathroom incident with Jennifer on her first day."

But I'm already curious. "Bathroom incident?"

"Hulk escaped during my bath last week," Henry explains with all the gravitas of an eight-year-old boy. "He went down the drain and Dad had to call the plumber."

Joshua nods. "That guy found three worms, two action figures, and a rubber duck. It cost Dad two hundred dollars to clean it all out."

I press my lips together to stop myself from laughing at Fletcher's mortified expression. "Well, at least Hulk survived his adventure."

"Yes! That's what I said!" Henry beams at me like I'm the first adult to understand his perspective.

The water begins to boil, and Fletcher adds the pasta with practiced efficiency. I watch him from the corner of my eye while I stir the vegetables into the chicken. His movements are confident despite his claims about kitchen disasters. Maybe he's being modest, or maybe having a nanny around makes him as if he needs to downplay his domestic skills.

"Can I set the table?" Charlotte asks, sliding off her stool.

"Absolutely, sweetie, that would be great." Other children I've lived with never would've asked that question. "Thank you, Charlotte. It was very sweet of you to offer."

As she bustles around gathering plates and silverware, I notice how naturally she takes charge of the task. She's clearly used to helping out, probably more than most eleven-year-olds would.

"Jennifer?" Amelia's voice is quieter than her siblings' and more hesitant. "Do you really know how to cook? Like, real food? Not just pasta and chicken?"

"Honey, I can make everything from scratch biscuits to beef bourguignon," I tell her. "My grandmother taught me to cook when I was about your age. And she taught my mother too."

Amelia's eyes light up. "Could you teach me sometime?"

"I'd love to." My heart swells at her request. It's the first genuine interest she's shown in connecting with me. That happened so soon, it warms my heart.

Fletcher watches our exchange with a tender expression that makes my stomach do a little flip. I command myself to concentrate on the pasta, which is nearly done.

"Five-minute warning," I announce. "Everyone, wash your hands before dinner, please."

For the first time in my entire career as a child caregiver, I feel like I might have found a family I can love.

And one hot daddy I should never, ever kiss again.

Chapter Nine

Fletcher

The children shuffle up the stairs toward the hallway where their respective bedrooms lie. Joshua and Henry share a room, as do Amelia and Charlotte. That's as it should be. Forcing my youngest daughter to sleep in the same room as my youngest son, the earthworm-lover, would be sheer torture for her. As the two doors click shut, a sigh of relief rushes out of me.

Now that we're alone, I slump down on the sofa opposite Jennifer. She chose the large armchair instead. As I let my head fall back against the thick cushions, a sigh rushes out of me. "Crikey. Two superhero movies in one night? That's a new sort of torture."

Jennifer grins. "What, you aren't a fan of *Superman*? The seventies versions were the best, if you ask me."

"You will never catch me wearing a skintight blue-and-red suit, and certainly never a cape."

"That's too bad. I think you'd look rather dashing in a cape." Jennifer wags her brows, and her eyes sparkle with mischief. "Very heroic, for sure. And you've got the right body for all that Lycra."

I splutter at her suggestion. "The children would never let me live it down."

"Really? I bet they'd insist you wear it to parent-teacher conferences."

The image makes me laugh despite my exhaustion. "Charlotte would write a four-page essay about superhero gender stereotypes. Joshua would try to build me a utility belt. Henry would demand I rescue his worms from imaginary villains."

"Amelia would design you a mermaid sidekick costume," Jennifer adds, tucking her legs beneath her in the chair.

I watch her settle into the large, puffy armchair that almost seems to swallow. "You handled them perfectly tonight. Dinner, homework, the bedtime negotiations, even the great toothbrush debate that we have every night."

"If toothbrushing is your biggest nightly battle, you're lucky," Jennifer says with a sweetly feminine laugh. "My last family had twins who would literally hide in the laundry hamper to avoid bedtime."

"I'm not sure luck has anything to do with it." I stare at her for a moment longer than I reasonably should. The way the lamplight catches her hair makes it glow like burnished copper. "Henry once flushed his toothbrush down the toilet because he was convinced it was possessed by evil spirits."

Jennifer's eyebrows shoot up. "Evil spirits?"

"Joshua told him the bristles moved on their own at night." I roll my eyes. "Cost me three hundred dollars for the plumber, and Henry slept in my bed for a week afterward."

"Poor little guy." Her expression softens, and something in my chest tightens in response.

Gazing at her, I wonder if Jennifer might become a permanent member of the household—at least until all the children have grown into adults and begun their own lives. Once that happens, Jennifer will have no reason to stay here with me. I don't want that, anyway. Marriage had given me only pain and frustration.

But Jennifer is beautiful and sensual. Every time she walks past me—in the upstairs hall, in the kitchen downstairs, or even in the car—the sweet scent of her arouses me. My cock decides now is the time for it to thicken and twitch inside my trousers. The memory of our one and only kiss rushes through me once more, and suddenly, I realize I'm breathing harder. *Bloody hell.* I need to fuck her immediately.

No, I will not do that. Shagging the nanny would make me a cliche of the worst sort.

Jennifer glances my way, dragging her tongue over her bottom lip. I'd swear she's staring at my cock. No, she wouldn't do that. I shift my position to hide my growing arousal and snatch up a throw pillow, placing it strategically on my lap.

"Are you okay, Fletcher?" Jennifer asks, her voice now a sensual whisper. "You look flushed."

"I'm knackered, that's all." What a bloody liar I am. "Sorry, that's not entirely true. I'm a bit...uncomfortable, but I am not exhausted. Not in the least."

Jennifer tilts her head, those green eyes boring into me with an intensity that only makes my condition worse. "Why are you uncomfortable? Because we kissed once and it was phenomenal?"

"I thought we agreed to forget about that."

"Well, I didn't get the memo." She slithers off the armchair, crawling toward me on all fours. Her fluidly graceful movements capture all my attention. "I don't recall agreeing to anything. Do you?"

Bloody hell. She is flirting with me, isn't she? I grip the pillow tightly, but that doesn't stop me from gawping at her tits. I can see the stiff peaks beneath her gauzy blouse, and suddenly, I realize, she must not be wearing a bra. Those luscious mounds bounce a little every time she adjusts her position in the armchair. My breaths grow faster and harder by the second, and I begin to feel as if a demon has taken over my body. Why else would I do the unthinkable—letting my cock seize control of my brain.

I slide off the sofa and onto my knees, crawling toward her until I'm mere inches away from that sexy body. When she leans toward me, her hair brushes against my cheek, silky and tantalizing. As I glide that hand up toward her breast, my cock becomes a steel rod in my trousers. Jennifer's chest is heaving, just like mine, and my mouth waters, as hungry for her body as I am for hers.

"Fletcher," she whispers, her voice huskier, "Pretty sure I know what you're after, but we can't...not here..."

"Yes, we fucking can." My knees are beginning complain about my awkward position, but I still can't move away from her. "I know it's wrong, but I just can't bloody force myself to stay away. Go to your room, Jennifer. Now. Otherwise, I guarantee I'll ravish you."

The aroma of her lust has grown thick and heady around us. The intoxicating scent is driving out all sensible thoughts. But suddenly, I remember the box of condoms I'd bought a few months ago in the desperate hope I'd meet a woman like Jennifer. And now I have met her, I should not seduce her. No, absolutely not.

But then she drags one fingertip down her chest, ever so slowly, until it meets the hem of her blouse.

My heart pounds, and I can barely breathe.

Jennifer grabs my shirt to yank me closer, our mouths almost touching now, her breaths teasing my lips. "I haven't been with anyone in two and half years. You're sexy as hell, Fletcher, and I want you so badly I think I might lose my mind."

Her confession unravels the last thread of my self-restraint. It shatters so thoroughly that I gasp and growl like a rabid beast, devouring her mouth, kissing her with all the pent-up lust that's been simmering between us ever since we met, only to burst free in this moment. She tastes like the wine we shared at dinner and something uniquely her. She fists her hands in my shirt more tightly while I deepen the kiss, and my cock has begun to throb painfully, desperate for me to plunge my length into her sheath.

"The children," I mumble against her lips.

"Don't worry, they're asleep in their rooms." She struggles to unhook the buttons on my shirt. "We'll be quiet. Besides, my attic room is the only thing on this floor."

I wrap my arms around her waist and hoist her up and into my arms. While I consume her mouth, she roughly explores my arse with her hands. How often had I fantasized about her luscious curves? Constantly. Her warm, voluptuous body presses against me, and the thin fabric of her blouse doing nothing to hide how much she wants this too.

"Upstairs," I snarl between kisses. "Now, Jennifer."

I make a brief detour to snag the box of condoms. While I whisk her up the stairs, she continues working at my buttons. We're acting like teenagers, unable to keep our hands off each other for even a second. She lashes her legs around my waist as I grind against her—and somehow keep trudging up the stairs while making very little noise.

"We shouldn't," she whispers, even as her hips rock against mine.

I groan, trailing kisses down her neck. "Tell me to stop."

"Oh god, Fletcher…" Her head falls back, exposing the delicate column of her throat. "Please, I need you inside me."

Her desperate tone does me in. I hold her close with one arm as I swiftly yet quietly whisk her upstairs to the attic door with trembling fingers. The stairs creak softly beneath our combined weight as I carry Jennifer into her attic room. My heart pounds so hard I'm certain she can feel it through my shirt. Her breath are seductively warm against my neck, and every step fires a heat-seeking missile straight to my groin. I can't hold out much longer.

"Fletcher, are you sure about this?"

I pause on the landing, gazing down at her flushed face. "I've never been less sure of anything in my life, pet. But I've also never wanted anything more. This hunger is both right and wrong, and I don't give a toss."

She reaches up to touch my cheek, her thumb tracing my jawline. "I don't want to complicate things for your family."

"You won't." The words come out rougher than I intend. "This is just us. Just tonight. Then we forget it ever happened."

Jennifer twists the knob for me, and I kick the door shut behind us—making barely a sound. We are alone. Completely alone. I set Jennifer down at the foot of her bed, my hands shaking as I fumble with the buttons of her blouse. Her fingers are steadier than mine, finishing the work she started on my shirt downstairs. When she pushes it off my shoulders, the cool air hits my bare skin, making me shiver. Maybe that sensation occurs only because she's gazing at me like I'm a delicious dessert she can't wait to consume.

"You're so fucking beautiful," I whisper, transfixed by the sight of her lacy bra. It's simple, practical even, but the way it cups her breasts makes my mouth water.

She glides her hands up my chest. "I've been wanting to touch you since this morning."

I groan and capture her mouth again, unable to resist the pull between us. Her blouse joins my shirt on the floor, and I press her down onto the mattress with its soft quilt beneath her. Before I know it, we're both naked. Her skin is like silk beneath my fingers as I trace the curve of her waist, the dip of her spine, the downy hairs between her thighs. I smell her cream. Fuck, I'll go mad if

I don't plunge my cock inside her. I need it so badly it's almost pathetic.

I trace the line of her collarbone with one finger, trailing kisses down to her navel. She arches her back, fisting her fingers in the pillow beneath her head.

"Hurry, Fletcher, please." Jennifer arches beneath me again. "Tell me everything you want to do to me. Please, Fletcher, now."

The invitation in her voice breaks something loose inside me.

"Blimey, you're a goddess, Jennifer."

The time for talk is over now. If I'm not inside her within ten seconds, I'll go stark-raving mad. So, I rip the condom box apart in my effort to grab one packet and roll it onto my rock-hard length. Then, I draw in a cleansing breath, grasp her hips and plunge my cock inside her slick heat.

Chapter Ten

Jennifer

The moment Fletcher thrusts into me, I let out a soft, husky cry of relief as my body lifts off the bed. The exquisite fullness robs me of breath. I moan, clutching his shoulders and digging my nails into his skin as the sheer joy of our joining hits me. "Oh god, yes! Fletcher, don't ever stop fucking me, not ever, not even if an asteroid slams down onto this house."

Fletcher's throaty chuckle makes me shiver in the best way. But suddenly, he freezes above me, his eyes wide and wild. "I need to take you like a filthy animal. Not sure how much longer I can hold back."

"Don't hold back," I beg, wrapping my legs around his waist. "I'm yours completely, do anything you want to me."

We both instinctively keep our voices as low as we reasonably can, given how intensely we want to devour each other. He groans again, his forehead dropping onto mine as he begins to move inside me. Every thrust goes deeper than the last, the friction both delicious and maddening. My body welcomes him as if we've done this a thousand times before.

"Christ, Jennifer," he snarls against my neck, his voice deeper and rougher. "I could die while fucking you, and it would be worth the pain."

I've lost all capacity to form words, and I can only whimper while he fills me up entirely. It's been so long since I've felt anything like this—raw need and desperate hunger that makes the entire world fade away. Fletcher's hands grip my hips, pulling me closer as he drives deeper.

"More," I gasp, my fingernails raking down his back. "I need more of you."

He growls low in his throat, the sound vibrating against my skin as his mouth finds my breast. He circles his tongue around my nipple before drawing it between his teeth, making me cry out softly. The dual sensations of his mouth around my nipple and his cock moving inside me threaten to shatter my control.

I can feel myself climbing toward an explosive climax, my body folding in on itself more and more while his thrusts grow wilder, more feral, like a werewolf claiming his mate. My juices dribble down my thighs and onto his skin. Fletcher seems to sense that I'm teetering on the edge, because he finds my clit with his thumb, rubbing it in merciless circles with just the right amount of pressure. The combination makes me fold in on myself even more, and I end up awkwardly placing my legs over his shoulders. I suck in a sharp breath, frozen as my climax crashes through me, my inner walls clenching around him while from screaming his name.

"That's it, love," Fletcher growls, his eyes locked on my face as I blow apart beneath him. "Let go for me. Do it now."

My inner walls are still pulsing around him when he flips us over in one swift motion. He clutches my hips with both hands, urging me to straddle him. The new angle makes me gasp, my sensitive flesh stretching to accommodate him even more deeply.

"Ride me," he commands, all but snarling the words. "I want to see those perfect tits bounce while you take whatever you want."

I plant my hands on his chest and begin to move, rolling my hips in a rhythm that makes us both moan and gasp. Fletcher's hands clamp onto my thighs hard enough to leave marks as I lift and lower myself on his thick shaft. His eyes devour me, dark with lust and something wilder.

"Oh shit, Fletcher, you feel so damn good," I pant, bearing down on him. "Don't stop, never stop, please, please, please."

He slides his hands up to my breasts, cupping them roughly. Then he brushes his tongue over my nipples in rhythm with my movements. I'm still sensitive from my first orgasm, and everything feels like too much—and also not enough. I throw my head back, losing myself in the sheer bliss of this moment.

Then Fletcher does something incredible. He sinks his teeth into the pliant flesh of my shoulder, and unbelievably, that sends me careening off the cliff. My second climax hits harder than the first, my body convulsing as waves of pleasure crash through me. I bite down on my lip so hard I taste copper, desperate to muffle the scream building in my throat. Fletcher's eyes roll back as my walls clench around him. With a muffled roar, he pulls me down hard against him, his cock pulsing as he finds his own release. The heat of it floods through me, marking me in the most intimate way possible.

We collapse together, both of us breathing hard as the aftershocks ripple through our bodies. Fletcher's arms wrap around me, holding me against his chest as we try to catch our breath. I can hear his heart hammering beneath my cheek, matching the frantic rhythm of my own.

"Bugger me," he whispers into my hair, his voice rough and satisfied. "That was..."

"Wow, you were incredible," I tell him while pressing a gentle kiss to his collarbone. The taste of his skin is salty with sweat. Damn, I want to lick every inch of him.

Fletcher strokes his hands up and down my spine, his touch gentle now in contrast to the desperate way he gripped me moments before. "We should probably talk about what this means."

I lift my head, noting the uncertainty flickering in his eyes. The vulnerability there makes my chest tighten with something that's dangerously close to affection.

"Do you want it to mean something?" I ask. "We're both adults. We both needed this. If that's all you want..."

Fletcher traces his thumb along my jawline, his touch so gentle it makes me want to melt into him all over again. "Is that what you want? For this to be purely physical?"

The honest answer terrifies me. I want so much more than just physical pleasure with this man. I want lazy Sunday mornings and shared jokes over breakfast. I want to be part of his children's lives as more than a nanny, to help Henry with his art projects and listen to Charlotte's feminist theories. I want to belong here like I've never belonged anywhere before.

But wanting those things too dangerous, too vulnerable, especially when I'm just beginning to find my footing in this household. "No idea what I want. But I know I don't regret this."

Fletcher's eyes search mine, and I feel naked in a way that has nothing to do with our lack of clothes. "I don't regret it either. But Jennifer—"

A soft thud from downstairs freezes us both mid-conversation. We lie perfectly still, barely breathing as we listen for any sign of children stirring.

"Probably the house settling," I suggest, but Fletcher is already disentangling himself from me, his movements quick and efficient.

"Can't risk it," he says, gathering his scattered clothes. "If one of them wakes up and finds their way to the attic stairs…"

"You're right, we should be more careful." I scramble to locate my underwear in the tangle of bedsheets. Fletcher's already stepping into his jeans, the muscles in his back flexing with every movement. I want to run my hands over every sinew one last time, to experience the strength beneath his skin, but the moment for that has passed.

"Time for me to go," he whispers, ditching the condom and buttoning his shirt with nimble fingers. "Thank you for this, Jennifer. It was unexpected yet bloody brilliant."

"Mm, it was amazing," I say, pulling my blouse over my head. "I hope things won't get awkward between us."

"Don't worry about that." Fletcher pauses, his hands stilling on the last button. He veers his gaze to mine, becoming abruptly serious. "We must be cautious, Jennifer. The children—"

"I know, I know." They come first, always." As I smooth down my skirt, I experience a *duh* moment. This is my room. I don't need to leave. "See you in the morning."

He smiles tightly, hesitating. Then he steps closer to cradle my face in his hands with a tenderness that makes my heart stutter.

And he walks out the door, shutting it softly.

I swallow against a lump in my throat, incapable of forming words.

Stripping off my clothes, I collapse onto the bed and curl up under the covers. The sheets smell like us—like amazing sex and sweat and something uniquely Fletcher. I press my face into the pillow and inhale deeply, trying to memorize his scent. Then the truth hits me like a cannonball.

What have I done? Screwing my employer? If Fletcher doesn't fire me, I'll hand in my resignation myself. Jeez, I've slept with my employer and crossed every professional boundary imaginable. Though I should feel shame for what I've done, somehow, I can't muster any disgust at my behavior.

Okay, this was a onetime thing. We were both stressed out and hadn't gotten any in so long that we were bound to erupt. I refuse to regret our encounter, but it cannot happen again.

Nope, never.

Unless Fletcher sneaks into my bed tomorrow night...I'll never summon the willpower to turn him away. Not if he aims that steamy smile at me. Or he kisses me. Or...anything.

Yeah, I'm doomed.

Chapter Eleven

Fletcher

Somehow, I manage to sneak back into my bedroom without waking any of the children. I also fall asleep quickly. Two miracles in one? My luck can't be that powerful. Thoughts of Jennifer naked plague my slumber, so yes, my good fortune has disintegrated. My dreams involve her writhing beneath me, shouting my name while I fuck her. Despite my tortured sleep, I still awaken refreshed. A bloody fantastic shag will do that to a bloke. I drag myself downstairs at half-past six, hoping the children haven't noticed my tardiness. The smell of bacon and eggs hits me as I round the corner into the kitchen, and I stop dead in my tracks.

Jennifer stands at the stove, her hair twisted up in a messy bun, wearing jeans that hug her curves in all the right places and a billowy peasant blouse that for some reason arouses me even more. She's humming cheerfully as she flips bacon, completely at ease in my kitchen. The sight sends heat straight to my groin and brings back vivid memories of last night.

I keep a discrete distance between us as I say, "Morning, Jennifer."

She glances over her shoulder, and our eyes meet for a brief, charged moment. "Good morning, Fletcher. I hope you don't mind that I started breakfast early. The kiddos will be down soon."

"I don't mind at all."

She smiles sweetly. "Grab a stool."

I move to the coffee pot, needing caffeine more than I need oxygen right now. My hands aren't entirely steady as I pour myself a cup, hyperaware of Jennifer's presence behind me. Once I sit down, the aroma of coffee begins to relax me.

"Did you sleep well?" she asks.

"Eventually." I sip my coffee, careful only to face her sideways and noticing that she carefully avoids looking directly at me too. "What about you?"

"Mm, I slept so well it ought to be a crime to feel so refreshed." She focuses intently on the sizzling bacon, but I detect a slight tremor in her hands as she moves the strips around in the pan.

We're both trying so hard to act normal that it seems anything but. I swear I can feel the unspoken tension while memories of tangled limbs and breathless moans hang heavily between us despite our careful politeness.

"Jennifer," I start, then stop. What am I meant to say? Thank you for the best shag I've had in years? Sorry I ravished you on your first day? Let's pretend it never happened and go back to being professional?

The thunderous noise of feet on the stairs saves me from having to finish that thought. Henry appears first, his hair sticking up at impossible angles, followed by Charlotte clutching a book about marine biology.

"Jennifer!" Henry shouts, launching himself toward her with extraordinary glee. "You're still here!"

I wince at his volume, but Jennifer simply laughs and ruffles his messy hair. "Of course I'm still here, sweetheart. I told you I was staying. You're stuck with me for a long, long time."

"The last nanny was gone before breakfast," Charlotte observes, settling onto a bar stool. "She left a note saying we were 'too much.'"

My chest tightens with familiar guilt. These children have been abandoned too many times—first by their mother, then by a parade of babysitters and nannies who couldn't hack it. Jennifer's words are like a balm to an old wound. What if she regrets making that promise after she's been here longer? No, I won't think about that. I can't.

"We are not too much for Jennifer. Mrs. Pennington was weak, that's all," Amelia declares dramatically as she sweeps into the kitchen with a blue streak freshly added to her hair. "She cried when Henry showed her his worm collection."

"Hulk isn't scary," Henry insists, climbing onto a stool next to Charlotte. "Jennifer likes him, don't you?"

Jennifer winks at him. "He's a very distinguished worm, honey."

I squint at my eldest child. "No more blue hair, Amelia. Wash it out now."

"But Dad," she whines.

"Get rid of it. Only natural colors are allowed in this house."

Amelia sulks but obeys my command, returning a few minutes later with damp hair that's no longer blue.

I watch this domestic scene unfold, struck by how natural Jennifer seems with my children. There's no awkwardness, no forced cheerfulness—simply genuine warmth. If only our own interactions could be as uncomplicated.

"Dad, you look weird," Joshua announces as he slouches into the kitchen, his clothes rumpled despite it being barely seven in the morning. "Are you sick?"

"Just, ah, tired," I mutter, taking a long sip of coffee and trying not to look at Jennifer.

"He's probably thinking about work stuff," Jennifer says smoothly, sliding perfectly cooked eggs onto plates. "Your dad works very hard to take care of all of you."

The grateful look she aims my way makes reminds me of what she looked like last night with her head thrown back in ecstasy. I grip my coffee mug tighter. It will probably shatter any moment.

"Can we have pancakes tomorrow?" Henry asks, bouncing slightly on his stool.

"If you eat all your breakfast today," Jennifer promises, setting his plate in front of him. "And if your daddy doesn't mind."

Amelia shakes her head in teenage disgust. "Henry wants pancakes every day of every week. I'd rather have something vegan."

Joshua makes a fake vomiting sound. "That's gross. We should eat eggs and bacon for the protein."

"There's nothing wrong with caring about what you put in your body," Charlotte adds, ever the diplomat. "But bacon does smell amazing."

"You said you're a vegan."

"No, I said maybe I'd like something vegan this morning. I still eat bacon and ham."

I watch Jennifer navigate this typical Murgatroyd family breakfast debate with impressive skill, neither dismissing Amelia's dietary preferences nor Henry's pancake obsession. She simply nods thoughtfully while plating the remaining eggs. "How about we plan a weekly menu together? Everyone can pick one breakfast for the week. That way Henry gets his pancakes, Amelia can choose something vegan, and Joshua gets his protein."

"What about me?" Charlotte demands.

"You get to help me plan the balanced meals," Jennifer says with a conspiratorial wink. "Someone needs to make sure we're getting proper nutrition."

Charlotte beams at being given such an important responsibility. I'm impressed by how effortlessly Jennifer has turned potential conflict into cooperation. It's a skill I've never quite mastered, usually resorting to bribes or threats when the breakfast debates turn into full-scale warfare.

"That's actually brilliant," I say, earning a quick smile from Jennifer that warms me on the inside.

The morning routine unfolds with surprising smoothness. Jennifer helps Henry find his missing shoe (under the sofa, naturally), reminds Joshua to pack his science project, and even manages to convince Amelia that she looks "perfectly beautiful" without additional coloring. I can't resist watching Jennifer, mesmerized by how she slotted herself into our disordered family dynamic overnight. She hasn't just adapted to it. She's improved it. The children are responding to her in ways they never have with any other caregiver. While we eat at the dining room table, the children discuss what everyone's day might be like. My little monsters might sometimes be a handful, but they never balk at helping clean up after a meal.

Then it's time for Jennifer to drive the kids to school. And that gives me a chance to relax briefly before I get dressed for work. All I do is sit in the armchair with my eyes closed, reveling in the silence. Then I dress quickly, trotting out to my car just as Jennifer returns from the school run.

She parks her car beside mine and gets out. The morning light catches copper highlights that shimmer in her hair, and I'm struck again by how sexy and lovely she is. How did I get so lucky? Hiring someone who looks like a goddess and can actually handle my children?

"How'd the drop-off go?" I ask, rolling down my window.

"Surprisingly calm. Henry made me promise to check on Hulk while he's at school, Charlotte reminded me three times about her soccer practice tomorrow, and Joshua asked if I know anything about hydraulics." She grins. "I told him we'd research it together tonight."

Of course she did. Another nanny would have deflected or made empty promises. Jennifer engages with their interests like they actually matter. "And Amelia?"

"Well, she asked if mermaids have to go to school in Atlantis. And if so, could she transfer there instead of going to a regular high school." Jennifer's eyes sparkle as she grins, her cheeks dimpling. "I told her we'd have to check on the admissions requirements."

I can't squelch my laugh. "You're going to fit in perfectly here."

"Certainly hope so." Her expression grows more serious, and I catch the faintest hint of uncertainty in her voice.

There's a moment of charged silence between us, the memory of last night hanging in the air like smoke. I want to say something about it, but not here in the driveway where neighbors might see us talking too intensely.

"I should get to work," I say reluctantly.

"Of course. I'll be here when you get home." Her tone of voice makes me horny. There's nothing overtly suggestive about her words, but the slight breathiness in her voice makes me think she's remembering last night too.

"Have a good day, Fletcher," she says softly, stepping away from my car.

I offer a tight smile and reverse out of the driveway. But I catch her in my rearview mirror, standing there watching me leave. The image burns itself into my brain—Jennifer in her peasant top, the morning sun creating a halo effect around her auburn hair.

The drive to the hotel passes in a blur of conflicted thoughts and emotions. I should regret what happened last night. I should establish clear boundaries between me and the nanny. I absolutely should not be fantasizing about bending her over the kitchen counter while my children are at school. Christ, I shouldn't be thinking about the way her velvety walls wrapped around me, the soft cries she made when I took her nipple into my mouth, and how perfectly our bodies fit together. I haven't felt this deeply connected to anyone for such a long time.

My phone buzzes just as I shut off my car in my assigned space. It's a text from Jennifer: *Hulk is safely in his dirt box. Henry forgot his lunchbox—it's in the fridge. Don't worry, I'll take it to school at lunchtime—J.*

As I stare at the message longer than necessary, I'm oddly charmed by the way she signed it with only her initial. Something about that simple "J" catches me off guard with its intimacy. It's like a secret between us.

So, I type back: *Thank you. You're already better at this than I am.*

Her response comes back quickly: *Just getting started. ;)*

The winking emoji makes my pulse accelerate. Is the nanny flirting? Or am I reading too much into a simple text? After last night, every interaction feels loaded with subtext.

I shove my phone into my pocket and head into the hotel, determined to focus on work instead of the gorgeous woman currently re-organizing my life in the most wonderful way possible. The Millbrook Grand's lobby bustles with the usual morning activity. Guests checking out, businesspeople grabbing coffee from our continental breakfast station, and my assistant manager Debbie waving frantically at me from the front desk.

"Mr. Murgatroyd!" she shouts, her voice carrying across the marble floor. "Thank goodness you're here. The reunion party for this weekend just called. They want to change the entire menu three days before the event!"

I sigh, pushing thoughts of Jennifer to the back of my mind. "Can't stand high school reunions and all the headaches they cause."

Debbie winces. "Oh, it's worse than that. This is a reunion of divorced couples who want to try swinging."

"We don't have any swing sets."

"That's not what 'swinging' means, Fletcher." She inches closer to whisper, "It means couples who want to, um, exchange partners. Like, sexually."

"Is that legal?"

Debbie shrugs. "Sex isn't illegal, unless you're doing it in public. Our guests will be discreet. Every couple does...whatever they intend to do, strictly in the confines of a hotel room. It starts in the ballroom, where everyone is clothed and they can, you know, choose their partners."

The things people do these days...

Oh yes, my life just keeps getting better.

Chapter Twelve

Jennifer

After another week of rough days at work, Fletcher arrives home at the usual time, collapsing onto the sofa with a look of sheer defeat in his eyes. I've given the kids the task of setting the table—partly to give Fletcher a break, but I would've directed the kids to set the table anyway. As soon as they came home, I had gotten them ready to do their homework.

I've never understood why children need to go to school for hours every day only to do more work at home.

Fletcher becomes more animated and cheerful as dinner goes on. Amelia rolls her eyes at him when he asks about her project for the science fair. She's been working on it for weeks, before I became part of the household. I know she's proud of her efforts, though she'd never admit it.

"It's fine," she says, with a teenage tone that somehow compresses a paragraph of attitude into two syllables.

"Just fine?" Fletcher presses, a hint of his old spark returning. "The way you've been hoarding the kitchen table for your volcano, I expected something more dramatic than 'fine.'"

"It's not a volcano," Amelia corrects him with exaggerated patience. "It's a sustainable energy demonstration. Mrs. Wilkins said it was college-level work."

I hide my smile behind my water glass. The girl is gifted. She reminds me of myself at that age, though with considerably more sass.

"And how was your day, Charlotte?" Fletcher turns toward the eleven-year-old who has been methodically arranging her peas into a smiley face.

"I made the soccer team!" Charlotte announces. "Coach says I have natural talent."

"That's brilliant, love!" Fletcher beams at her. The pride in his eyes is unmistakable.

"We should celebrate," I suggest. "Maybe ice cream after dinner?"

Fletcher shoots me a grateful look.

I shrug like it's nothing, but warmth spreads through my chest. It's strange how quickly I've settled into this routine with them. Three weeks ago, I'd never even met these people, and now I'm planning their celebrations. But it feels right somehow.

"Ice cream?" Henry pipes up from his end of the table, where he's been suspiciously quiet. "Can I have chocolate with rainbow sprinkles?"

"With fudge sauce and caramel too," adds Charlotte, her soccer victory apparently deserving of maximum toppings.

Fletcher raises an eyebrow at me. "You've opened Pandora's Box now."

"I can handle it." But honestly, I'm not positive about that. I've never lived with so many kids before.

After dinner, I drive us all to the ice cream parlor on Main Street. It's one of those charming small-town spots with a striped awning and handwritten flavor boards. The kids tumble out of the car like they've been released from incarceration after years of confinement.

"Slow down," Fletcher calls out after them, but they're already at the door, pressing their faces against the glass like they've never seen ice cream before.

"You'd think they were starved at home," I say as Fletcher and I follow at a more reasonable pace.

"The Murgatroyd sweet tooth is legendary," Fletcher explains, his hand briefly touching the small of my back as he holds the door. "My mum used to hide the biscuit tin on top of the fridge. I'd use a broom handle to knock it down."

The ice cream parlor is bustling with families enjoying the warm evening. Fairy lights twinkle from the ceiling, and the sweet scent of waffle cones fills the air. I breathe it in, surprised by how much I'm enjoying this little outing. Henry is already chattering away to the teenage server, who looks both amused and overwhelmed by his detailed ice cream order. Amelia hangs back, pretending she's too mature for this kind of childish excitement, but I catch her eyeing the mint chocolate chip.

"What would you like, Amelia?" I ask.

She shrugs. "Whatever."

I nudge her gently. "Afraid 'whatever' isn't a flavor last time I checked."

A hint of a smile cracks her carefully constructed teenage indifference. "Fine. Mint chip. In a cup, not a cone."

"Good choice." I step up to the counter. "One mint chip in a cup, please. And I'll have..." I scan the flavors, deliberating. "The lavender honey, single scoop."

Fletcher raises his eyebrows. "Adventurous, eh?"

"I'm not always buttoned up, you know." I wink before I can stop myself.

I catch a flash of something in his gaze that I can't quite identify. Interest? Surprise? Whatever it is, it makes my pulse quicken.

"I'm a woman of mystery," I add, trying to sound casual.

Fletcher laughs. "That you are, Jennifer Cordell. That you are."

The way he says my name makes my tummy flutter. But I focus on paying for our order while Fletcher wrangles the children into a booth by the window.

"Can I try yours?" Charlotte asks as I slide in beside her, careful not to spill my lavender honey scoop.

"Only if I can try your mint chip."

"Yours tastes like Grandma's soap," Charlotte declares, wrinkling her nose.

I laugh. "That's the sophisticated palate talking."

The sun has sunk lower in the sky, and the kids are getting sleepy. Joshua insists he's wide awake. When I see Amelia yawning, I know it's definitely time to go home. Fletcher insists on tucking the kids in himself once we get back to the house, and I love that he takes such care with his children. He's a good father. No it's more than that. He's an incredible dad.

Fletcher sidles past me, accidentally brushing his arm against mine. A faint shiver rushes over my bare arm. Yes, okay, I want to have sex with him again—but I won't do it. My job is to take care of the children and the household in general. Heck, I even dug out a steam cleaner I'd found in a closet downstairs and gave the whole house a good cleansing while no one else was around.

When the weekend comes around again, things get super hectic in the Murgatroyd household. Fletcher's parents and in-laws, who live in the same general neighborhood, finally decide to pay us a visit. What if they hate me? No, they won't. I'm sure they're wonderful people. But I've never lived in a household where two sets of grandparents lived nearby.

We don't receive any notice of their impending arrival. They simply ring the doorbell and wait until Fletcher waves for them to come inside. The kids are thrilled, naturally.

I plaster on my most professional smile as they file in—Fletcher's parents first, followed by his ex-wife's parents. Talk about awkward. I'm suddenly very aware of my casual outfit—jeans and a light sweater that seemed perfectly appropriate for a Saturday at home but now seems woefully inadequate.

Fletcher walks over to me and settles a hand on my shoulder. "Let me introduce you to these lovely people, Jennifer." He points toward each parent in turn. "These two are my parents, Florence and Edmund Murgatroyd. And the other couple are Claudia's parents, Patricia and Robert Sullivan."

"It's wonderful to meet you all," I say, extending my hand. "I'm Jennifer Cordell."

Florence Murgatroyd is a petite woman with silver-streaked hair—and sharp eyes behind her wire-rimmed glasses. She gives me a once-over, like I'm being scanned by airport security. "And what exactly is your role here, Miss Cordell?"

Fletcher jumps in before I can answer. "Jennifer is our new nanny. She's been a godsend for all of us."

My throat tightens at that statement. A godsend? That's going a little overboard. But I keep my head up and offer my hand to Florence. "I'm so glad to meet you, Mrs. Murgatroyd."

She sweeps her gaze over me, her brows lifting. When she finally shakes my hand and speaks, her British accent is no surprise to me. "Well, dear, I must inform you that I can tell a person's character with one glance."

"How did I do?"

Florence winks and grins. "You can call me Florry. As for Fletcher, I've never seen my son this relaxed before. I've also never known my grandchildren to behave like such perfect little angels. Fletcher is right. You are a godsend."

Before I have a chance to respond, the other set of grandparents marches up to me.

I paste on a pleasant smile. "It's wonderful to meet you too, Mrs. Sullivan."

"Oh no, dear, don't call me Mrs. Sullivan." She kisses my cheek. "Everyone calls me Patty. That includes you, Jennifer."

My cheeks have grown slightly warm. "Oh, um, thank you. I appreciate—"

A burly man wearing a wide grin seizes me, strapping his arms around me in a big hug. Fortunately, he pulls away before I suffocate. "Aren't you a pretty little thing! Fletcher told us you're amazing with the kids, but he didn't mention how gorgeous you are."

I'm pretty sure my face just flushed completely red. "That's very kind of you to say, Mr. Sullivan."

"Call me Bob!" He claps Fletcher on the shoulder. "Son, you hit the jackpot with our girl."

Fletcher clears his throat. "Right, well, shall we all sit down? I'll put the kettle on."

"I'll help," I offer quickly, desperate to escape the scrutiny of four sets of parental eyes.

The kitchen becomes a refuge. Fletcher busies himself with mugs while I hunt for cookies in the pantry—or biscuits, as Fletcher would say. I hear the kids in the living room regaling their grandparents with wild stories. I've noticed Fletcher likes to spout tall tales too, so it must be a family trait.

"Your parents are terrific," I tell him, trying to fill the awkward silence.

"They are. And Bob and Patty are good people too, despite everything." He pauses, his hand hovering over the teapot. "Despite what happened with Claudia, they never blamed me. They still treat the kids like their own grandchildren."

"That's...unusual." I arrange cookies on a plate, trying to make them look fancy or...something. "Most in-laws aren't so forgiving when their daughter leaves."

Fletcher's eyes cloud over momentarily. "Claudia's choices were her own. Bob and Patty understood that better than anyone. She's their daughter, after all."

I want to ask more questions, but this isn't the time. Instead, I reach for the milk jug, accidentally brushing Fletcher's hand. That same electric current zips through me, and I pull back too quickly, nearly dropping the milk.

Fletcher snags the milk jug, setting it on the counter. "Careful there, Jennifer."

"Sorry. It was slippery."

He holds my gaze a beat too long. "Very slippery indeed."

The way he spoke those words fired an erotic shiver down my spine, settling between my thighs.

The kettle whistles, breaking the tension. Fletcher turns away to deal with it, but I can still feel the heat radiating between us. *Get a grip, Jennifer. You're supposed to be professional.*

I know I should behave that way. But the longer I live with Fletcher and his kids, the harder it is to remember that I'm not the woman of the house.

Chapter Thirteen

Fletcher

Once all the hugs are over with, and two sets of grandparents have settled down to sit on the sofa, the children do calm down somewhat. Unfortunately, the settling down only lasts for a few minutes. As long as the grandparents keep talking, everything seems normal and reasonably calm. They want to hear all about what the children did at school today. No one pays attention to me or Jennifer for a blessed but short hiatus.

Then the conversation dwindles. I attempt to fill in the silence, but I'm ruddy awful at casual conversation. So, I fumble around to find something—anything—to say. "Would you senior citizens like to go for a walk with us? It's a lovely afternoon. And since this is the weekend—"

Henry jumps up from his chair, waving his hands as if he's directing air traffic. "No walks! Not boring walks! We should play cricket!"

I freeze. Cricket? Where did that idea come from?

"Uh, cricket?" Jennifer says. She looks as confused as I am. "You want to play with insects? I thought worms were your thing."

I rub my forehead. "Since when are you interested in cricket, Henry?"

"Since forever!" His conviction is endearing. "Grandpa played it in England, right? He told us all about it. They can teach us!"

"You understand that cricket is a sport, Henry, don't you?"

Mum's eyes widen, and she shoots me a horrified look. "Yes, it's an awfully violent sport for children. Don't you think, Fletcher?"

My father grins. "Oh, don't be such a spoilsport, Florry. I've still got my old bat in the car. Never go anywhere without it."

I stare at my father, shaking my head. "You actually keep a cricket bat in your car? I had no idea."

"Mostly for emergency situations," he says with complete seriousness. "But you never know when you might need one for a spontaneous match."

Jennifer covers her mouth, but I can see her shoulders shaking with suppressed laughter. At least someone finds my family's eccentricities amusing.

"I don't know the first thing about cricket," Patty admits cheerfully. "But I'm willing to learn."

"But I don't remember the rules," I declare, though I bloody well do remember. I can't have the children messing about with cricket bats, not until they're adults. Thirty would be my preference. But everyone, including the grandparents, is getting more and more excited about the idea.

Bollocks. I must stop them. And so, I blurt out an alternative without considering the ramifications. "Perhaps we should go to the new water park. It's right here in Millbrook Valley."

The children instantly start shrieking and jumping around like lunatics.

"Are you serious, Dad?" Henry asks while pumping his fists in the air.

I've made a terrible mistake. The look of pure joy on Henry's face tells me there's no backing out now. The water park also has various rides and fun foods. Its sole purpose seems to be to separate parents from their money while subjecting them to migraine-inducing levels of noise and general bedlam. "Yes, well, I suppose we could. Provided we can find our swimsuits—"

"YES!" Charlotte shrieks, jumping up and down.

Amelia grins, and it's a genuine, unguarded smile that transforms her entire face. "Can we really go, Dad?"

"Yes, why not," I hear myself saying, though I swear I can already feel dollar bills vanishing from my wallet. "It'll be fun for everyone."

Jennifer throws me a look that clearly says, *are you completely nuts?* But she's still smiling. "I should probably mention I don't actually own a swimsuit."

"We can stop at a store on the way," Patty suggests helpfully. "I need one too. Haven't been swimming in ages."

"Right then," Dad says, rubbing his hands together. "Adventure it is! Though I still think cricket would've been more civilized."

"Cricket is boh-ring," Henry announces with the confidence of someone who's never actually played the game. "Water slides are wayyy better."

I catch Jennifer's eye and mouth at her, *I'm sorry.* She shakes her head, but she's smiling as she whispers to me, "The things you'll do to avoid cricket."

She walks past me to help Charlotte find her swimsuit.

"You're coming too, aren't you, Jennifer?"

"I wouldn't miss it for the world," she confirms. "Though I hope you realize you've unleashed a monster. They'll want to go to the water park every weekend now."

"One crisis at a time." I watch as my mother begins listing all the potential dangers of water parks while simultaneously helping Henry locate his swim trunks.

An hour later, after a chaotic stop at a department store, we finally arrive at our destination. The children are practically vibrating with excitement. The parking lot is absolutely packed, which should have been my first warning. The second warning comes when we hear the screams—not screams of terror, but the gleeful shrieks of hundreds of children having the time of their lives.

"Crikey," I mutter under my breath.

Mum gawps at the massive water park complex with the same expression I imagine I'd wear if someone told me I had to wrestle a crocodile.

Jennifer emerges from the car wearing a stunning new sundress, a plastic shopping bag clutched in her hand. I try not to think about what's in that bag. But I fail spectacularly.

"All right, you monsters," I announce with false cheer. "Everyone ready for some fun?"

The children don't reply. They're already racing toward the entrance like they've been shot from cannons. I hurry after them while

Mum trails behind, muttering about proper queuing etiquette and health regulations.

"Fletcher, wait up!" Jennifer calls, her voice barely audible over the cacophony of splashing water and delighted screams.

I turn back to see her struggling with her bag and purse while trying to keep up. Without thinking, I clasp her hand to help her navigate through the crowd. Her fingers are warm and soft against mine, and I hold on longer than strictly necessary.

"Thanks," she breathes, slightly out of breath. A few hairs have escaped from her elegant style, and I have the ridiculous urge to tuck it behind her ear.

"Dad, hurry up!" Henry shouts from somewhere near the entrance turnstiles. "The lines are getting longer!"

I reluctantly release Jennifer's hand, and we push through the throng of families. The admission fee makes my stomach drop to the floor, but the kids' excitement is infectious enough that I hand over my credit card without too much grumbling.

"This place is mental," I whisper to Jennifer as we're swept along by the crowd toward the changing rooms.

"You're the one who suggested it," she reminds me, but she's grinning. Her cheeks are flushed from the heat and excitement.

"Temporary insanity brought on by cricket-related panic."

The changing rooms are chaos incarnate. I help Henry into his swim trunks while trying to keep track of where everyone else has gone. Dad emerges looking surprisingly fit for his age in navy swimming shorts, while Mum appears in what can only be described as a swimming costume from nineteen-fifty-two, complete with a ruffled skirt.

"Very fetching, Mum," I tell her.

She sniffs. "It's practical, dear."

I'm about to respond when Jennifer emerges from the women's changing room, and my brain short-circuits completely. She's wearing a simple black one-piece, but there's nothing simple about how it hugs every curve of her body.

"Is this appropriate?" she asks, tugging self-consciously at the neckline. "It was the only one they had in my size that wasn't covered in flamingos."

"It's perfect," I say, my voice embarrassingly hoarse. "Very…suitable."

Dad elbows me in the ribs. "Close your mouth, son. You're catching flies."

I snap my jaw shut. Jennifer's cheeks flush pink, and she busies herself with arranging her clothes in a locker.

"Right. Where are the children?" I ask, desperate to change the subject.

Henry has already claimed the tallest water slide and is dragging Charlotte toward it while Amelia pretends she's not interested in the Wild-Wild River ride. I spot them weaving through the crowds of sun-soaked families.

"There," I point toward the towering monstrosity known as The Water Coaster, which Henry seems determined to conquer. "Though I'm not entirely sure I want to follow."

Jennifer laughs, a sound that somehow cuts through the chaos around us. "Come on, it'll be fun. When's the last time you did something completely ridiculous?"

"This morning—when I suggested coming here."

She bumps her shoulder into mine. "Don't be a spoilsport. The kids are having a great time. Isn't that the whole reason we came here? To act as silly as the children?"

"Maybe," I say slowly. "But with six adults and four children to wrangle, this might turn into an apocalyptic disaster. I can picture you and me and the grandparents getting arrested for child endangerment because we let them try to most frightening ride in the park."

Jennifer smiles gently and sighs. "A place like this has rules and safeguards. They'd never stay in business otherwise."

"So, you're telling me to stop being such a stick in the mud. Correct?"

"Yep." She slips her arm around mind. "Give it a try, at least. What do you say, Fletcher?"

The last thing I want to do is become a crotchety old man before I'm even forty. But…

Jennifer leans dangerously close to me, whispering in a sultry tone, "You're not fooling me, Mr. Murgatroyd. I've experienced your wild side firsthand. Unleash it again now, but in a family-friendly way."

She's spot on, of course. I've tamped down my wilder instincts simply because I am a father. But here in this ridiculous water park, I suddenly realize I want to get crazy with my kids.

Chapter Fourteen

Jennifer

We have all put on our swimsuits at last. The joyful screams and shrieks of Fletcher's children make my heart swell. I can tell by his expression that his heart's about to burst too. His grin encourages me to do the same, and I love seeing him this way. An adventure at a place like this might change everything for this family—and for me.

Fletcher shakes his head as Josuha sneaks up behind Charlotte to surprise her. Then Fletcher turns to me. "I've been too stand-offish, I can see that now. But I have no reason anymore to pretend I don't want to leap into the water cannonball style just like my children, and even the grandparents, have done."

He aims a wicked grin at me, then does exactly what he suggested.

Fletcher Murgatroyd, the always calm single dad, takes a running start toward the pool and launches himself into the air with the most spectacular cannonball I've ever seen. The splash is enormous. Water erupts in all directions, soaking nearby sunbathers who shriek and laugh.

When he surfaces, gasping and grinning like an idiot, the kids are staring at him with their mouths hanging open. "I haven't done that since I was twelve!"

"DAD!" Henry screams with pure delight. "DO IT AGAIN!"

Even Amelia is laughing unabashedly as she wipes water droplets from her face. "I can't believe you just did that, Dad!"

"Your father's gone completely mad," Florence declares, but she's smiling too.

I dip my toes into the water, lingering at the edge of the pool. "That was quite the entrance, Mr. Murgatroyd."

"Oh, I'm just getting started. Try a cannonball, pet. It's invigorating."

His new attitude has infected me too. I scuffle backward, then sprint toward the edge of the pool, leaping into the water to execute my own cannonball. The cold water hits me like an electric shock, but when I surface, I'm laughing harder than I have in months. Fletcher has a playful glint in his eyes as he splashes me.

"Not bad for a nanny," he teases.

"I'll show you what 'not bad,' really means." Then I launch myself at him.

Suddenly, we're embroiled in an all-out water war. Henry trots up beside us and unleashes whooping battle cries as he dunks his father. Charlotte joins in, ganging up on me with surprising stealth. Even Amelia wades over, pretending she's too cool to participate while secretly splashing Joshua when he's not looking.

"This is a madhouse!" Patty laughs from the shallow end where she's been watching our antics.

"Absolute bedlam," Robert agrees, but he wades in anyway, making his way toward us with the determination of a man half his age.

The ruckus escalates when Edmund produces an inflatable beach ball. "Water volleyball, anyone?"

"Where did that even come from?" I gasp, treading water beside Fletcher.

"My father is mysteriously prepared for everything," Fletcher quips, his wet hair plastered to his forehead in the most ridiculously attractive way. "I've stopped questioning it."

Henry immediately claims the ball, hugging it to his chest like it's made of gold. "Teams! We need teams!"

"Kids versus adults!" Charlotte shouts.

"That's hardly fair," I protest. "There are more of us."

"Yeah, but we're faster," Amelia exclaims with a smirk that reminds me exactly where Henry gets his mischievous streak.

Fletcher moves closer to me, his arm brushing mine in the water. Droplets cling to his eyelashes. "I'll be on your team, Jennifer."

The sultry tone of his voice sets off a fluttering in my stomach. I clear my throat. "Good. I'm extremely competitive."

"Are you now?" His eyes dance with amusement. "That doesn't surprise me one bit."

Before I can respond, Henry is shouting about positions and rules he's clearly making up on the spot. The pool has become our battlefield, with the inflatable ball flying back and forth over an imaginary net.

Florry hovers at the edge, perching primly on a deck chair, reluctant to join in the madness. "I'll keep score."

"Oh no you don't," Fletcher says, wading over to her. "Everyone plays."

To my shock, he gently but firmly pulls his mother into the water. She exclaims "oh!" and sputters, her carefully styled hair now dripping wet.

"Fletcher Ralph Murgatroyd!" she gasps, but there's laughter in her voice. "You absolute menace!"

I watch in amazement as prim and proper Florry starts to giggle—actually giggle—while she adjusts to the water temperature.

Fletcher's grin is triumphant. "There's the Mum I remember."

Henry seizes the moment of distraction to lob the beach ball directly at Fletcher's head. It bounces off with a satisfying thwack.

"Point to the kids!" Charlotte cheers, pumping her fist in the air.

"That wasn't even a proper serve!" I protest, lunging for the ball as it floats past me.

"All's fair in water volleyball," Amelia declares with teenage authority.

I snatch the ball and hurl it back at the kids' side of the pool. It smacks Henry squarely in the chest, and he lets out an exaggerated "oof!" before dissolving into giggles.

"Jennifer's ruthless!" Fletcher announces with obvious admiration.

"I warned you I was competitive."

"You did indeed." He's watching me with something that looks suspiciously like desire. Water streams down his chest, and I force myself to look away from his hot body.

"My turn!" Florry calls out, surprising everyone. She paddles over with determination, her prim demeanor completely abandoned. When Henry tosses her the ball, she serves it with surprising accuracy.

"Bloody hell, Mum!" Fletcher exclaims as we all scramble to return her shot.

"Language!" she scolds automatically, but nobody believes she's angry.

Our entourage makes the rounds of the best and most fun places in the park. Then we head out to find food, sampling the eats at three of the best vendors. We adults insist on making the children let their food settle before we move on to other exciting places within the water park.

Fletcher's youngest son takes off for parts unknown in this massive park.

"Henry, wait!" I holler after him, but he's a blur of excitement darting through the crowd.

Fletcher sighs beside me. "So much for letting our food settle."

"I've got him," Amelia says, jogging after her younger brother. "Charlotte, come on! You too, Josh!"

The four of them disappear into the throng of wet, sunscreen-scented bodies while Fletcher and I exchange glances with the grandparents.

I gather our scattered belongings. "I suppose we should follow them."

Florence dabs at her damp hair with a towel. "I think I'll sit this one out, dears. These old bones have had quite enough excitement for one day."

"Nonsense," Fletcher declares, taking her hand. "You were brilliant on the Murgatroyd water volleyball team. I'm not letting you quit now."

She protests weakly, clearly, she's secretly pleased. She has a twinkle in her eyes that wasn't there this morning.

We make our way through the maze of attractions toward the Go-Karts. The afternoon sun beats down on my shoulders, and I'm grateful for the frequent misting fans scattered throughout the park. As Fletcher walks beside me, I catch hints of chlorine and something distinctly him beneath the sunscreen.

"Your mother's having the time of her life," I observe as Florry chatters excitedly with Patty about her volleyball prowess.

Fletcher grins. "She is, isn't she? I haven't seen her this relaxed since…well, since before Claudia left."

The mention of his ex-wife creates a brief tension between us. I want to ask more, but I won't push it. This day is too perfect to ruin with heavy conversations. "Everyone's having fun. That's what matters."

We reach the Go-Karts just as Henry is trying to convince the operator he's tall enough to drive his own kart. Fletcher steps in before his son can stage a full-on rebellion.

"You can ride with me, champ," he suggests, ruffling Henry's hair.

The boy pouts for approximately two seconds before excitement takes over again. "Can I steer sometimes?"

"We'll see." Fletcher winks at me in a way that suggests the answer to Henry's query is absolutely not.

Amelia has already gotten in line, playing the blasé teenager but clearly eager to get behind the wheel. Charlotte bounces beside her, while Joshua is eyeing the track with a mix of excitement and trepidation.

"Want to be my co-pilot?" I ask.

Joshua's face lights up. "Really? You'd let me ride with you?"

"Absolutely." I smile at his enthusiasm. "We'll be the dream team."

He high-fives me with enough strength that I nearly lose my balance. Fletcher catches my elbow, giving me a sly wink. His breath tickles my ear. "Careful there, love. Can't have our star driver injured before the big race."

I turn to face him, acutely aware of how close we're standing. "Planning to eat my dust, Murgatroyd?"

"Oh, so that's how you want to play it, hmm?" He lets out a barely audible throaty chuckle. Then he moves toward his eldest son. "Joshua, I hope you're prepared for defeat. Henry and I are unbeatable."

"In your dreams!" Joshua shouts, grabbing my hand and pulling me toward the line.

The Go-Kart track unfolds before us like a miniature highway, complete with twists and turns that make my pulse rev up. The smell of rubber and gasoline mingles with the chlorine still clinging to my hair.

"First time?" the college-age operator asks as he helps Joshua and me into our karts.

"I'm an old pro," I fib smoothly, buckling Joshua in beside me. The truth is, I haven't been in a Go-Kart since my university days, but I'm not about to admit that to Fletcher.

Two karts down, Fletcher waging his own battle while trying to get Henry properly secured. The boy keeps trying to climb into the driver's seat while Fletcher patiently redirects him to the passenger side. The kids love the Go-Karts, and I wind up playing driver for Charlotte and Amelia too. At first, Amelia pretends it's all a dumb kiddie thing. But quickly, she starts having as much as fun as the children.

I might not have known these children for long, but already I adore them. As for Fletcher...Our hot night in my attic room changed things between us in ways I've tried not to think about.

But for how much longer can I ignore the obvious?

Chapter Fifteen

Fletcher

After our crazy, wonderful day at the water park, Jennifer and I drop the boys off at my Mum and Dad's house and then leave the girls at Patty and Bob's home. It seemed like an equitable arrangement. The change of venue had been my idea. I'm too bloody knackered to deal with the children tonight. And besides, both sets of grandparents wanted the whole rest of the weekend with the boys and girls. Naturally, they'll have joint outings too.

Jennifer drives us both home—but then suggests that she should take a room at the Millbrook Grand for the weekend.

I want nothing of the sort. So, as we pull into the driveway and Jennifer switches off the engine, I twist toward her. "You will do no such thing, Jennifer. This is your home now too."

"Yeah, but I don't think it's appropriate."

"Rubbish." I lean toward her until my lips brush her cheek. "This might be the only chance we'll have to spend time together alone. Simply talking, or even…something naughtier."

Her eyes flare wide briefly. "Oh, I see."

"The choice is yours, darling. What do you want?"

Her throat works as she swallows, gripping the wheel tighter. Then she turns to face me. "I want *you*, Fletcher. Every inch of that sexy body. On top me, inside me, kissing and fondling me then finally making me come for you."

My heart hammers, and my breathing grows ragged. "The things I plan on doing to you are absolutely filthy."

"Oh god, Fletcher, please do filthy things to me. The dirtier the better."

I clasp her hand. Lift her fingers to my lips. Kiss every knuckle slowly. "Let's go inside. Right now."

As we jog to the front door, my hands begin to shake, and I fumble with the keys.

"Fletcher, please hurry."

The sultry tone of her voice drives me mad.

I spin round, and she's right there. Close enough that I could kiss her. But that will wait until we're safely ensconced in the house.

"Kiss me," she whispers. "I need your tongue tangling with mine *right now.*"

"I'd rather devour your cream. And the aroma of it is already intoxicating me."

Can't wait one second longer. My mouth finds hers. Soft at first. Tentative. Then she makes a small sound in the back of her throat, and something inside me snaps. I crush her against the door as my tongue tangles with hers. She tastes like every decadent food on earth—sweet and addictive. Her hands fist in my shirt while she drags me closer. Somehow, I get the key to work and stumble through the doorway with Jennifer in my arms.

I kick the door shut behind us, pushing her against the wall.

She thrusts her tongue into my mouth with a ravenous hunger that makes me growl and grunt.

"Hurry, Fletcher. I've wanted this for so long, I can't hold back much longer."

"Neither can I."

She's right. I've been fighting this attraction ever since our first forbidden encounter. How many times did I tell myself it was inappropriate, and we can't do it again. She deserves better than a knackered single father with more baggage than Heathrow Airport. But right now, with her hands on my chest and her lips swollen from my kisses, I've forgotten why I was fighting it.

I lift her blouse over her head, dropping it onto the floor. She's wearing a pale pink bra that nearly translucent. Her breasts are perfect, full and soft and begging for my mouth on them.

"You're so fucking beautiful, Jennifer."

Pink blooms on her cheeks, and that blush is the sexiest thing I've ever seen. I love watching her blush like that while my cock is buried inside her so deep that I'll know she's mine. Completely mine. Maybe we should chat first, or perhaps have a sandwich. *No, you bloody moron, get naked and make her scream for you. Do it now.*

I sweep her into my arms, surprising her with a low grunt of effort. Once she locks her arms lock around my neck, I carry her toward the stairs and take them three at a time. My bedroom's just down the hall. So, I kick the door open with my foot, not bothering with the lamp.

The moonlight spilling through the window is enough, and I lay her down on my bed. Jennifer reaches behind her back to unhook her pink bra, tossing it away. The garment lands on the floor halfway across the room. The rest of her clothes go next. Her luscious tits are even more beautiful than I remembered, full and perfect, with nipples that make my mouth water. I drag my tongue over my lips as I reach for her, desperate to taste her skin again.

But Jennifer as other ideas.

"Your turn, Big Daddy," she purrs. "Strip, Fletcher. Now."

I fling my shirt away, and it flutters to the floor. Then her hands are on my chest, exploring every ridge and valley. I shut my eyes and let myself feel every sensation. Her soft fingers explore me while I try to unzip my trousers. My hands are trembling, which makes it difficult to undress, especially with Jennifer virtually salivating when she gazes at my cock. But with Herculean resolve, I finally ditch my trousers. Next, I awkwardly get rid of my underwear, nearly ramming my elbow into Jennifer in the process. Only after I've completed that task do I realize I'm still wearing my shoes and socks.

"Fletcher, look at me. Please. Let me see every inch of that incredible body." She smirks as her focus shifts down to my groin. "No dad bod here, that's for sure."

Jennifer gazes at me reverently as if I'm some sort of miracle. Like I'm not simply a knackered single father with gray creeping into his hair and worry lines etched around his eyes.

Her gaze travels down my body, halting at my groin. "Let me tell you just how hot you are."

Before I can protest, she's kissing my chest. Working her way down with her tongue until she finds one of my nipples. I hiss in a sharp breath as she takes it between her teeth.

"Bloody hell, Jennifer."

She smiles against my skin. "I like the way you say my name when you're losing control."

My hands find her hair. Tangle in the soft strands. "You haven't seen me lose control yet."

I flip us around until she's the one against the bed. My mouth finds her throat. I taste salt and something uniquely her. She arches beneath me, pressing those perfect breasts against my chest.

"Fletcher, please."

I must slow down and make this good for her. But when she whispers my name like that, all rational thought flies out the window.

My hands work at the button of her jeans. She lifts her hips to help me slide them down her legs along with her knickers. Pink lace that matches her bra. Christ, she's gorgeous. Every inch of her.

I kneel between her legs, drinking in the sight of her. Her chest rises and falls rapidly. Her green eyes are dark with want.

"You're staring," she breathes.

"Can't help it." My voice comes out rough. "You're perfect."

I lean down to kiss her stomach. She shivers beneath my lips. Her hands find my hair, tugging gently as I work my way lower. When I reach the edge of her knickers, I look up at her.

"Tell me what you want, Jennifer."

"Everything." Her voice breaks on the word. "I want everything with you."

I hook my fingers in the pink lace and slide it down her legs. She's bare before me now, and I've never seen anything more beautiful in my entire life.

"Fucking hell," I breathe.

She reaches for my belt. Her fingers fumble with the buckle, and I cover her hands with mine to help. My trousers hit the floor, followed by my boxers. Now we're both naked, and the air between us crackles with electricity.

I lean down and crush my lips to hers again, thrusting my tongue deep, curling it around hers. She tastes like want and need and everything I'd been denying myself for months before Jennifer walked into my life. Her hands roam my body, leaving trails of fire everywhere she touches.

She moans, and eyes flutter half shut as she slides her hand down to my cock.

"Once we do this, everything will change. The first time we made love, we could brush it off as momentary madness. But this time..."

"It'll be more than just a hot fuck," she says, her words mirroring my thoughts. "But I already feel a connection between us, the kind that's deeper than lust."

That's all I need to hear. I sheath my cock with a condom and position myself between her creamy thighs and thrust into her, hoisting her legs onto my shoulders as I plant my hands at either side of her hips. Once I begin to move inside her, I slow things down, taking my time so I can watch her expressions as I fill her up. She's tight and wet around me, and I can't hold back for much longer.

Her eyes flutter shut as her lips curl into a blissful smile. A soft moan spills from her lips, their color now a darker shade of pink. Her tits shiver every time I thrust into her.

"Open your eyes, Jennifer. Watch me thrusting into you."

Her green eyes open, locking onto mine as I sink deeper. The connection between us is electric. Sacred, even.

"You feel incredible," I breathe against her ear. "But I can't take it slow for much longer."

She wraps her legs around my waist, pulling me closer. "Go for it, Fletcher. Make me scream."

I begin thrusting in earnest, faster, harder, wilder than ever before. I can't think anymore, too caught up in our intensely erotic shag care about anything else. The bed creaks and bounces while Jennifer shouts incoherently, something about my "huge, hot dick" and how much she loves it. When I hit just the right spot, she thrashes her head and releases more incoherent sounds. I growl when she digs her nails into my shoulders. I know I'll wear those marks like badges of honor.

"Faster, Fletcher, faster!"

I pick up the pace. She meets my every thrust as I struggle to stop myself from hyperventilating. My ears are ringing, but I don't give a toss. Her tits bounce wildly, and her back arches so high that she might fly out into space. I struggle against the need to spill myself inside her before I've given her everything I have. She will come first. I'll make certain of that.

When Jennifer wraps her thighs around my hips, I'm gone. Her heels dig into my back, urging me deeper, and I drive into her with pure abandon. The wet sucking sound of our bodies colliding fills the air—along with the scent of her cream.

"Fletcher," she cries out. "Oh god, Fletcher, please don't stop!"

"Sorry, I—have to—stop—eventually."

I'll have a heart attack if I don't come right now. Her walls clench around me, and I know she's on the edge too. I slide my hand between us, finding that sweet spot with my thumb and circle it slowly, deliberately.

"That's it, love. Come for me, Jennifer. Come for me now and don't stop until I say so."

Chapter Sixteen

Jennifer

Fletcher's command that I must come immediately doesn't seem like it ought to do the trick—but it does. I shatter beneath him once again, my body arching off the bed as I cry out his name. Waves of pleasure ripple through me as Fletcher holds me steady, his strong hands anchoring my hips while I thrash and cry out his name over and over. Once the orgasm has faded, I'm still gasping, still coming down from that high when he groans against my neck, his breath hot and ragged.

"Bloody hell love," he growls. "You come like a supernova."

I sink my fingers into his shoulders while aftershocks pulse through me. I've never felt so exposed, so vulnerable, yet so completely safe at the same time. Fletcher's gaze holds mine, dark and intense, pupils blown wide with desire.

"Your turn, Fletcher." I reaching between us to sink his cock deep into my velvety channel.

His expression has turned feral, as if he wants to devour me like a craven beast. Fletcher freezes for a moment, then slams his dick into me so hard that a sharp cry bursts out of me. As he begins pummeling me, I realize I'm completely at his mercy. The intensity of his movements shifts something fundamental between us—this isn't just physical anymore. This is Fletcher claiming me, marking me with his body, and that both terrifies and thrills me. I never could've imagined the calm, collected single dad would turn ravenous.

But I love it.

Every thrust shoots lightning straight into my core. I wrap myself around him, plunging his cock deeper inside me, needing every inch of him to fill me up. The headboard slams against the wall in an erotic rhythm, and the bed thumps on the floor, but I don't care who hears. The sounds flesh on flesh fill the room, and the way he grits his teeth while grunting does something to me I'd thought was unthinkable.

He makes me come again.

This time the climax hits me so powerfully that I scream. "Oh god, Fletcher! Yes! Yes! Don't stop, never stop!"

He finds my clit with his thumb, rubbing it mercilessly while he consumes my nipple too. The dual sensation has me spiraling toward another peak embarrassingly fast. I sink my teeth into his shoulder to keep from screaming too loudly. I might scare the couple next door.

The pleasure has become almost unbearable—too much and yet not enough. But just as Fletcher punches into me one last time, another orgasm shudders through me. He throws his head back and howls like a werewolf, frozen in his final thrust.

Then he gets rid of the condom and flops onto the bed beside me on his back. His eyes flutter shut, and his chest heaves. Now that we're both spent, I sprawl on my back, dazed and exhilarated in equal measure.

"Jennifer, pet, you've given me the best sex in the entire universe." He brushes his fingertips over my cheek. "Sounded like you experienced something just as incredible. Am I right?"

"Oh god, yes, it was beyond description." I aim a sloppy smile at him. "You are a sex god, Fletcher Murgatroyd. Your parents should've named you Eros."

He chuckles. "I appreciate the compliment, but I'm hardly a god."

I roll over onto my side, slinging my arm across his chest. "After that workout, you need to feed me."

His sweetly lopsided smile melts my heart. "I think we both need to replenish our energy some savory foods. How does that sound?"

"Mm, yes. You read my mind."

Fletcher sweeps me up in his arms and carries me down to the kitchen. I'm naked and being carted around by an equally naked Fletcher, yet somehow, it's totally natural. His strong arms enfold me, and I know he would never let me fall. I listen to the steady thrum of his heartbeat against my ribs.

My thought a moment ago wasn't quite right. I have fallen—but not physically.

"You do realize I can walk," I remind him.

"Where's the fun in that? Besides, after the workout I just gave you, I'm not entirely sure your legs would cooperate."

He's not wrong. My thighs are still trembling from the aftermath.

Soft evening light bathes the kitchen. Fletcher sets me gently on the cool granite countertop, and I shiver at the contrast against my heated skin.

"Are you cold?" he asks, already moving toward the refrigerator.

"Maybe a little." I swing my legs, watching the play of muscles across his back and shoulders as he moves. Fletcher's body is a work of art, sculpted and strong in ways that turn me on like crazy. "I can't believe we're doing this. A naked midnight snack after body-shattering sex. It's very rom-com of us, don't you think?"

Fletcher opens the fridge, ducking his head in there. He emerges again holding a block of cheese and cold cuts. Then he hunts down a bottle of wine. "Nothing wrong with being a cliché if it feels this bloody good."

He grabs two glasses from the cabinet, his body stretching in the sexiest way. I'm sore in the most delicious way possible, yet I'm already wondering how soon we can go back to bed.

"See something you like?" He catches me staring, a knowing smirk playing on his lips.

"Maybe." I try for nonchalance but fail miserably. "Scratch that. The answer is yes. I love your body and especially that amazing dick."

He pours us each a glass of deep-red wine and hands one to me. Our fingers brush during the exchange, igniting little sparks on my skin.

I take a sip, letting the wine warm my throat. "So tell me something I don't know about you."

Fletcher leans against the counter opposite me, completely unselfconscious in his nakedness. "What would you like to know, darling?"

"Everything." The word comes out more breathlessly than I intended. "I mean, we just had the most incredible orgasms of our lives, and I realized I don't even know your middle name."

"Ralph." He assembles a small plate of cheese and crackers. "Fletcher Ralph Murgatroyd. Rather stuffy, isn't it?"

"I think it's damn sexy. Sounds like a proper British gentleman who becomes a maniac in the bedroom." I accept the cracker he offers, biting into it as I mumble, "What else?"

He cups his hand around his ear in a sarcastic manner. "Sorry, love, what did you say? Your chomping drowned out the words."

I roll my eyes. "Crackers aren't that loud."

He pops a piece of cheese into his mouth, chewing thoughtfully. "All right, here's something you don't know. I wasn't always this calm and collected. Back in my twenties, I was quite the hothead. In my university days, when I played cricket, I was known as the Terminator."

"You? The Terminator?" I laugh, nearly choking on my wine. "I don't believe it."

"Oh, but it's true. I got into more pub fights than I care to admit. My ex-wife used to say I had a temper like a caged animal." His expression darkens slightly at the mention of her. "But later on, I realized she was egging me on because she loves a good fight between blokes."

"That makes more sense." I set down my glass and clasp his hand. "What happened with Claudia? I mean, if you want to talk about it."

Fletcher traces circles on my palm. "Claudia left. She said motherhood wasn't what she'd signed up for, and she needed more adventure and excitement than I could provide. She missed the brawls I used to get into."

"That's horrible." I reach out to touch his cheek. "Your brawling days are over, and it's all because of your children, isn't it? They must have changed your life."

"Oh yes, they did. I wouldn't want to live without them."

Something in his voice breaks my heart a little. The fierce protectiveness, the way his whole face lights up when he mentions his children. This man transformed himself completely for those kids. I've grown to love them too, almost as much as Fletcher does.

"Tell me a bit more about *you*, Jennifer. I know you're from Arkansas, but not much else."

His voice pulls me out of my thoughts. "My life back home was pretty simple. I started out working with kids who'd been through trauma, trying to help them process their experiences. I was good at it, but work took an emotional toll on me. That's why I switched to being a nanny." I take another sip of wine and let the liquid courage loosen my tongue. "I think I'm good at it, but I always feel like something's missing. Like I'm helping everyone else build their families while mine remains a distant dream."

Fletcher steps closer, positioning himself between my legs. His hands rest on my thighs, thumbs stroking lazy patterns on my skin. "And now?"

"Now I'm sitting naked in a kitchen with the sexiest man I've ever met, talking about feelings." I laugh, shaking my head. "If you'd told me six months ago that this would be my reality, I'd have rushed to the nearest therapist to get my head shrunk."

"Therapy might not be a bad idea," he says with that dry British humor. "We're both clearly mad."

"Speak for yourself, Mr. British Hottie."

His laugh is low and husky. "British Hottie? That's a new one."

"Would you prefer Sexy Brit? English Stud Muffin?" I grin, emboldened by the wine and the post-orgasmic bliss. "I have a whole list in my head."

"Please, no more." He feigns horror, then smiles again. "I admit I'm curious about this list."

"I'm afraid it's a trade secret." Leaning forward, I drop a soft kiss on his lips. He tastes like wine and cheese. "Your turn for confessions, Big Daddy."

He slides his hands higher up my thighs. "What sort of confessions?"

"The deep, dark kind. Tell me something that would shock me."

Fletcher's expression grows more serious. "I used to think I was broken after Claudia left. That maybe I was the kind of man who drove women away. That I'd never be enough for anyone." His voice drops to barely above a whisper. "But with you, tonight…Christ, Jennifer. You make me feel like I'm worth something again."

My heart clenches at the raw vulnerability in his words. I cup his face in my hands, forcing him to meet my gaze. "Fletcher, you are worth *everything*. Claudia was an idiot to leave you and those beautiful children."

He leans into my touch, closing his eyes for a moment. "I never thought I'd feel this way about anyone again. You've turned my world upside down, pet."

"Good." I pull him closer until our foreheads touch. "I like your world better upside down."

He grins. "So do I."

Chapter Seventeen

Fletcher

After the intimate conversation Jennifer and I had last night, something quite unexpected happened. I wanted to sleep with her. No sex. Just sleeping in the same bed with our arms wrapped around each other. It was the most wonderful thing I've experienced. Now, I wake to sunlight streaming through the curtains and Jennifer's lush body molded to mine. Her head rests on my chest, and one arm lies draped across my stomach. Her breathing is delicate and feminine—until she lets out a sharp snort.

Even that piglike sound enchants me.

But I'm treading through unknown territory. Waking up with a woman in my bed hasn't happened in years. Not since before the divorce. But with Jennifer lying beside me, it seems completely natural.

She stirs against me, emitting a small moan that goes straight into my cock. Without opening her eyes, she drapes one arm over my chest and purrs, "Morning, sex god."

Her hair is a mess, and there's a crease on her cheek from my chest. I've never seen anything lovelier. "Sleep well, darling?"

"Better than I have in months." She stretches like a cat, and the movement presses her bare breasts against my ribs. And she smirks. "Guess you didn't notice what I said."

"If you mean the 'sex god' comment, I heard it all right." I chuckle, sliding my fingers through her silky hair. "But I simply can't believe a woman called me such a thing."

Jennifer props herself up on one elbow, giving me a spectacular view of her naked body.

"Fletcher Murgatroyd," she says in a cheeky scolding tone while tracing a finger down my chest. "I am completely in my right mind when I say you are absolutely mind-blowing in bed."

I seize her wandering hand and bring it to my lips. "If that's the case, perhaps we should verify your assessment. For scientific purposes, of course."

"Scientific purposes?" Laughter bubbles out of her. "Is that what the kids are calling it these days?"

I flip her onto her back in one smooth motion, hovering above her. "I'm quite serious about my research."

Her laughter fills the room, bright and clear and infectious. But then her expression shifts to something more serious.

"Fletcher." Her voice drops to a whisper. "What happens now?"

The question hits me like a punch to the gut. Because I don't bloody know what happens next. I've been so focused on getting to this moment that I haven't thought beyond it.

"What do you mean?" I ask, though I know exactly what she means.

"The children will be back tomorrow. We can't exactly reveal that their nanny is now screwing their father."

I wince at her bluntness, even though she's right. "We'll figure it out."

"Will we?" She searches my face. "Because I realize this isn't just some weekend fling for you. I can't do casual either, Fletcher. Not with you. Not when it involves the children."

My throat tightens. She's asking for promises I'm terrified to make. As I stare down at her beautiful face, framed by that wild hair, my heart thumps faster. The vulnerability in her green eyes terrifies me more than any commitment I've ever made.

"Jennifer, love..." I brush a lock of hair from her cheek. "This isn't casual for me. Nothing about us has ever been casual."

Relief flickers across her features, but she's not letting me off that easily. "Then what is it?"

I roll onto my side, pulling her with me so we're facing each other. Her naked body pressed against mine makes it difficult to think clearly, but this conversation is too important to cock up.

"Don't know what to call it yet," I admit. "But I know I want you here. In my bed. In my life. In the children's lives."

"As what? Your live-in girlfriend who happens to care for the children?"

The word "girlfriend" sounds odd to me. It's too casual, too temporary. But I can't bring myself to say anything heavier. Not yet. "I don't want you to be just the nanny anymore. "I want you to be…mine."

She searches my face. "Yours? What, like I'm your secret lover?"

"Christ, that came out wrong." I scrub a hand over my face. "I'm ruddy awful at this, aren't I?"

"Don't be so hard on yourself. You're doing fine." She traces her fingers along my jawline. "Please tell me what you're thinking. *Really* thinking. Please, Fletcher."

I capture her hand and press it flat against my chest, over my racing heart. "I'm thinking I've never felt like this before. Not even with my ex-wife. I'm thinking you're the best thing that's happened to this family in years. And I'm thinking I'm absolutely terrified of fucking it up."

"I get that, Fletcher, I do." Jennifer kisses my knuckles tenderly, one by one. "Even if our relationship doesn't work out, I would never abandon you that way, running off to another continent with a gigolo."

Of course she wouldn't. Jennifer Cordell isn't that sort. But the fear still lives in my chest like a cold stone.

"I know you wouldn't do that," I admit quietly. "But knowing something logically and feeling it emotionally are two different things entirely."

She shifts closer, her bare leg sliding between mine. "Then let me prove it to you. Day by day. Month by month."

The simplicity of her offer undoes the knot in my stomach. "You don't need to prove anything to me. But want to prove that I trust and respect you as more than a nanny."

"I fell in love with all of you, Fletcher. The father, the children, this chaotic beautiful life we've built together. I'm not going any-where."

My breath catches. "You love me?"

She taps my nose with one finger, smiling sweetly. "Did I not mention that last night when you had me screaming your name?"

"You might have been a bit incoherent at the time." I grin, rolling her onto her back. "I believe I was saying something along the lines of 'Oh Fletcher, yes, right there, don't stop, oh my god, I love you and your dick too.'" She mimics her own breathless voice, then dissolves into laughter. "Not exactly a Shakespearean declaration of love."

I lean down and brush my lips against hers. "Say it again. Properly this time."

Her smile softens. "I love you, Fletcher Murgatroyd. Every grumpy, gorgeous, devoted inch of you."

And that's when it happens. The dam inside me bursts. "I love you too, Jennifer. Have done since the day we met."

"Same for me. Never experienced love at first sight before, so is took me awhile to accept my feelings."

I kiss her feverishly, as she smiles against my lips. The heat between us builds again as if it will never cool down completely. Though our lust has reignited, instead of making love again, we pull on our night clothes and spend another hour just talking and laughing.

Yes, I do love Jennifer—and she loves me.

That means I should tell the children that their nanny has become my girlfriend. How will they react? I especially worry about Amelia. My eldest has always been the most protective of our family unit. She's taken on far too much responsibility since her mother left.

I frown at the ceiling. "Amelia will be the hardest to convince. She adores you, but switching from nanny to girlfriend might be a difficult transition."

Jennifer sighs. "I know. Amelia is a smart girl, and she's going to think I've betrayed her trust. She's fifteen, Fletcher. Everything is a catastrophe at that age."

I kiss Jennifer's forehead. "We'll need to be careful when we tell them. Start with the younger ones first. Prepare the ground before we tackle Amelia. Henry would be the most likely to think it's wonderful that you and I are a couple."

Jennifer nods. "Yeah, I agree."

"Charlotte's too young to understand the nuances, so she'll need special treatment." I gnaw on my lip while I contemplate the other children. "Joshua might be a problem. He already has a slight crush on you, but it isn't anything serious. He loves your waffles more than more than anything else."

"That leaves Amelia." Jennifer's voice grows quieter. "I don't want to lose her trust, Fletcher. We've built something special."

I pull Jennifer closer, inhaling the scent of her hair. "We'll find a way. Together."

That word hangs between us. *Together.* It feels both terrifying and exhilarating. Then my phone buzzes on the nightstand. I groan, reaching for it blindly. "If that's work, I swear to god—"

"It's your mother," Jennifer says, peering at the screen. "She's sent a text."

I squint at the screen. My mother's message is typically cryptic: *Boys having wonderful time. Made pancakes shaped like dinosaurs. Henry ate seven. Joshua complained they weren't scientifically accurate. Ring you later.*

Jennifer read my Mum's text too. I told her she should.

I shake my head, setting the phone aside. "Henry would eat dinosaur-shaped cardboard if you put syrup on it."

Jennifer laughs. "And Joshua would write a dissertation on why the stegosaurus plates are anatomically incorrect."

"Exactly." I kiss the top of her head. "At least they're having fun. That gives us more time to mull over how to break this news without causing a family revolt."

Jennifer traces lazy circles on my chest. "Maybe we're overthinking it. Children are more resilient than we give them credit for."

She's right, and I'm sure everything will work out with the children.

Chapter Eighteen

Jennifer

The day after Fletcher and I declared our love for each other, we resolve to bite the bullet and tell the kids everything. First, however, I need to help Fletcher calm his nerves. He isn't exactly neurotic about the situation, but he is, well…let's just say a swig of brandy wouldn't go amiss. Fortunately, he bucks up faster than I expected. No booze necessary. When I suggested last night that the grandparents should all be here for the big reveal, Florry took over the logistics of the operation.

Fletcher receives another text from his mom just as we're both ready for whatever might happen. His lips curl into a sweet smile.

I lean over his shoulder. "What did Florry say?"

"Mum told me she and Patty got the kids all dressed and ready for our 'big talk' as she calls it." He shows me his phone screen, and I can see Florry has added a string of thumbs-up emojis. "She's also reorganized the pantry and alphabetized the spice rack."

"Your mother's nervous energy is quite productive."

"Oh, you have no idea. Last time she was anxious about something, she color-coded everyone's sock drawers." Fletcher pushes his hand through his hair, making it stand up adorably. "Are we ready for this?"

"As I'll ever be."

We wait in comfortable silence, his hand clamped around mine. The warmth of it grounds me. When we hear the crunching of gravel in the driveway, I spot four little faces pressed against the backseat windows, instantly disappearing when they spot us looking.

Fletcher tightens his grip on my hand. "Here we go."

The front door bursts open before we can even reach it. Henry barrels toward us, followed by Charlotte and Josh, with Amelia bringing up the rear.

"Jennifer! Jennifer!" Henry throws himself at me. "Grandma Patty made pancakes and they looked like dinosaurs!"

"Mine was a stegosaurus," Charlotte announces, rolling her eyes.

I just see Fletcher over the kids' heads. He looks like he might be sick, the poor man.

"Shall we all go inside?" My voice is slightly higher than usual. Nerves, I guess.

Florence appears in the doorway, looking immaculate despite the early hour. Behind her, Patty wipes her hands on a tea towel, flour still dusting her shirt. The grandfathers shuffle in last.

"Everyone's here," Fletcher mumbles, his voice cracking slightly. "Smashing."

I usher the kids into the living room, trying to ignore the butterfly convention happening in my stomach. Florence has, of course, arranged the seating to perfection—children on the floor with cushions, grandparents on the sofa, and two chairs positioned front and center for Fletcher and me. It's a bit like we're about to perform in a very intimate theater production.

"Did we do something wrong?" Josh asks, his face scrunched with worry.

"Not at all," I quickly reassure him, leaning over to his level. "We have some exciting news to share, that's all."

Fletcher winces. "Right. Yes. Exciting news."

He's gone pale.

I lean back in my chair, reaching over to clasp his hand. "Your dad and I wanted to tell you something special."

The children all lean forward, eyes wide and bright with excitement. Josh's worry transforms into curiosity.

Charlotte grins. "Is it a puppy?"

Fletcher winces. "No, pet, it's not. Though that would be easier to explain."

I nudge him gently with my elbow. He's not helping.

"The thing is," I continue, "your dad and I have become very close while I've been helping your family."

"We know that," Amelia states matter-of-factly. "You're always looking at each other funny. We might be kids, but we aren't stupid. Well, except for Henry."

"Hey!" the youngest Murgatroyd exclaims with pouted lips. "I'm smarter than anybody except Jennifer."

Out of the corner of my eye, I see Patty trying to suppress a smile.

Fletcher dives right in. "The strange looks are, ah, because…Jennifer and I care about each other very much."

"Like friends?" Henry asks, tilting his head.

"Not quite." Fletcher scratches his cheek, wincing again. "We're more than friends. It's more like…ah, grown-ups who care for each other."

Poor Fletcher. He really sucks at delivering important news. The room goes quiet, and I can hear my pulse pounding in my ears.

Charlotte sits up straighter. "You mean like boyfriend and girl-friend?"

"Um, yes, like that," I admit, my cheeks burning hotter than ever. I expect my hair to catch on fire at any moment.

Josh scrunches his nose. "Are you going to get married and have smelly babies that throw up all the time? I remember when Henry was like that. It's gross."

Henry scowls at his brother. "Hey! I was never gross or smelly."

Fletcher's hand goes rigid in mine, and he stammers while attempt-ing to explain the situation. "We're getting a bit far afield here. Can we stick to the issue at hand, please?"

Josh nods and shrugs. "It's cool with me."

Amelia worries her lip. "But you might have babies?"

I wave at the grandparents, hoping for assistance, but they're no help. Florry and Patty look like they're doing their best not to laugh. The grandfathers seem as if they'd rather be anywhere else on earth.

"Babies?" Fletcher makes a strangled sound. "That's…well, something adults discuss privately."

Charlotte crosses her arms. "That means yes. I'm not cleaning up baby doo-doo."

"We haven't talked about that yet," I tell her, shooting Fletcher a sideways glance. His face has gone from pale to slightly green.

Henry bounces on his cushion. "I want a baby sister! Can you make one with purple hair?"

"That's not how babies work," Josh says, rolling his eyes.

"How do they work, then?"

Fletcher's grip on my hand becomes painful. I can practically hear his internal panic.

"The important thing," I nearly shout, trying to steer this runaway train back on track, "is that your father and I love each other and we want all you kids to feel comfortable having me as your father's girlfriend. You all mean so much to me."

Fletcher finally musters the courage to take control of the situation. "We want to know what you think about this change."

The room falls silent as four pairs of eyes stare at us. My throat feels as dry as the Sahara Desert.

"Does this mean Jennifer will live here forever?" Charlotte asks, her expression unreadable. "And you'll share Dad's room?"

Fletcher glances at me. "Not right away, no. But eventually, that's something we might consider."

I hold my breath, watching their faces carefully. Josh seems indifferent, studying a loose thread on his sock. Henry beams with excitement, probably still thinking about purple-haired babies. But it's Amelia and Charlotte who worry me most.

Amelia stands up suddenly, her arms crossed. "So, you're not going to leave like Mom did?"

The room goes dead silent. Even Henry stops bouncing. My heart clenches as I note Amelia's defiant stance, her chin jutted out like she's preparing for battle. Behind that tough exterior, I can see the scared little girl who watched her mother walk away.

"Oh, sweetheart." I stand up and take a step toward Amelia. "I'm not going anywhere. Ever."

"Will you pinky swear?"

"I'll do more than that." I wrap my arms around her. "I promise no one will ever take me away from you. I'm here for good, forever."

The children still seem skeptical, and I don't blame them.

But The situation is spiraling out of control. I caused this mess, and it's up to me to fix things. I love Fletcher, and he loves me. But the children matter more than our feelings. I adore these kids, but they need time to decide whether they're okay with me becoming more than the nanny. My throat chokes up briefly, then I rise and face the kids who are clearly scared.

"I have an idea," I say to everyone in the room. "You guys need time to process what we've told you. So, I'll get a room in the Millbrook Grand. That'll let you all talk about it for as long as you need to."

Fletcher jumps up. "Jennifer..."

I touch his arm. "This is for the best. Call me whenever your family has made a decision." I struggle to hold back tears. "You kids mean so much to me, and I never wanted to hurt you."

The room has gone as silent as a tomb.

I grab my purse and shuffle out of the house, hesitating on the threshold for two seconds before I shut the door behind me. My car is still parked along the curb. The drive to the hotel feels like it takes a thousand years, but I manage not to cry—until I walk into the hotel and finally shut the door to my room behind.

God, what if the best thing I can do is to walk away? That would destroy me. I've come to love those children so much.

I drop my purse on the floor, flop onto the bed facedown, and cry.

Chapter Nineteen

Fletcher

My children have mutinied. They seem intent on hoisting me up on their mast to hang pirate flag above me. That way, the crows can devour me more easily—or perhaps a killer whale will claim me first. All right, maybe I am exaggerating the situation for dramatic effect. But I have not lied about my children being quite angry with me. They switched from crying and/or pouting at me a moment ago. And their indignation stems from one specific event.

Jennifer is no longer in the house. She's at a hotel—*my* hotel. This is not how I imagined my Saturday would play out.

Amelia once again lifts her chin and crosses her arms over her chest. "Dad, you're an idiot."

My jaw drops. "I beg your pardon?"

"You heard me." She plants her feet wider, every inch the formidable teenager I've raised. "Jennifer just told us she loves us and wants to be part of our family forever, and you let her leave."

Charlotte nods vigorously beside her sister. "She looked really sad when she left."

"I didn't let her do anything," I protest weakly. "She made that decision herself."

"Because she thought we didn't want her!" Henry wails, his face still blotchy from crying. "But I do want her! I want her to stay and make pancakes and read me stories!"

Josh pounds his fists on a sofa cushion, his lips pursed. "And Jennifer promised to help me build that volcano for science class. The real kind, not the baking soda kind."

My jaw drops even further, and I flap my head like a ruddy cartoon character. "You lot were very upset. But I did *not* want Jennifer to leave. She felt it was the best thing she could do so that you four and I could discuss the situation."

Children, particularly *my* children, often change their minds at the speed of light. I should know better than to be surprised by their rapid emotional reversals.

"We don't want to talk about it unless Jennifer is here," Amelia proclaims. "She's part of the family now, and she should be here for family meetings."

Mum clears her throat, sitting serenely in an armchair. "Perhaps the children have a point, Fletcher. Jennifer did seem rather upset when she left."

"She was trying to protect us," Charlotte adds, with wisdom beyond her years. "But we don't need protecting from her. We need protecting from you making stupid decisions."

I run my hands through my hair, completely out of my depth. "So, what exactly are you suggesting I do?"

"Go get her!" all four children shout in unison.

Henry jumps up and tugs on my sleeve. "Tell her we want her to come home. Tell her we love her too!"

My kids might be insane, but they're very clever too. I had assumed they were upset because they found out Jennifer and I are in love. But no, that's not what was going on at all. What a bloody fool I am. They simply needed time to grasp the situation.

I stand here gaping at my children as if I've stepped into an alternate dimension where everything is topsy-turvy. One minute my children are devastated, the next they're unified in their demand that I fetch Jennifer back immediately.

"You're all absolutely certain about this?" I ask, needing to be certain before I make a complete arse of myself. "Because fifteen minutes ago, Amelia, you were—"

"Ugh, I was confused," Amelia interrupts, her voice softer now. "But that doesn't mean I don't want Jennifer here. She's different from Mom. She actually cares about us."

I step closer to Amelia and kiss her cheek. "Yes, love, Jennifer does care. Very much."

"Then why are you still standing here?" Charlotte demands, hands on her hips in a perfect imitation of her grandmother.

I raise my hands in surrender and pray the grandparents will support, but they're all nodding encouragingly. Even Dad gives me a thumbs up from his corner chair.

"That's it, then." I clap my palms together, decision made. "I'm going to fetch Jennifer."

My proclamation causes the children to erupt in cheers that nearly deafen me. Henry does a little victory dance while Josh pumps his fists in the air. Even Amelia allows herself a small smile.

"Hold on, you pirates," I raise a finger, "you lot are coming with me. This is a family decision, so we'll deal with it as a family."

"Road trip!" Charlotte shouts, already heading for the door.

I smile and shake my head. "The hotel is only fifteen minutes away. Your excitement is overblown."

Mum stands up, smoothing her skirt. "We'll wait here, Fletcher. This is something for you and the children to sort out."

Within minutes, I'm herding four excited children into the car. The drive to the hotel is chaos incarnate—Henry chattering nonstop about what he's going to say to Jennifer, Charlotte debating the best way to apologize, and Josh explaining the scientific method of winning someone back. Yes, teenagers think they know everything about everything. Amelia sits quietly in the front passenger seat, but I catch her checking her reflection in the side mirror—a sure sign she's nervous.

Once we've reached the parking lot, Amelia asks, "What if she doesn't want to come back? What if we've ruined everything?"

I park the car and turn to face the four of them. Their faces are a mixture of hope and worry that makes my chest tight.

"Then we'll respect her decision," I explain to them honestly. "But we'll also make sure she knows exactly how we feel. All of us."

Henry unbuckles his seatbelt with the determination of a soldier heading into battle. "I'm going to hug her really tight so she can't leave again."

"That's kidnapping," Josh points out.

"No, it's love," Charlotte argues, swatting at her brother. "Right, Dad?"

I blow out a sigh as we climb out of the car. "It definitely isn't kidnapping, Josh. But let's not smother her either. We need to be respectful."

"What's our plan?" Amelia asks, suddenly all business. "We can't just barge into the hotel and start yelling her name."

She's right, of course. I hadn't thought that far ahead, so focused on getting to Jennifer that I didn't consider how exactly we'd find her. "I suppose I should call the front desk and ask for her room number."

Josh points toward the hotel entrance. "Or we could just go inside and ask."

Simple solutions from the mouths of babes. I herd my brood across the car park, trying to maintain some semblance of order.

Henry marches alongside me. "Dad, this is your hotel. Can't you just use your special key? I mean, the one that lets you get into any room? You've done that before, right? I remember you told us about it."

The hotel lobby is mercifully quiet as we approach the front desk. The receptionist glances up with a polite smile that falters slightly when she sees my entourage of children trailing behind me.

"Good afternoon," I begin, adjusting my collar. "I'm looking for Jennifer Cordell, a good friend of ours. She checked in a little while ago."

The woman taps on her keyboard. "I'm sorry, sir, but we can't give out guest information without their permission."

I whip my badge out of my pocket and flash it at the woman. "You must be new here. I'm Fletcher Murgatroyd, the general manager."

"Oh! Mr. Murgatroyd, please forgive me. This is my first day on the job." Her face flushes pink as she starts typing frantically. "Miss Cordell is in room 237."

"Thank you, love. You're an angel."

She blushes even more, gazing up at me through her lashes. "Happy to help, sir."

"Just call me Fletcher." I turn to my children, who are all grinning. "Right then. Up we go."

The ride to the second floor seems to take an eternity—despite lasting only thirty seconds. Henry starts bouncing from foot to foot again, while Charlotte practices what she's going to say under her breath. Josh examines the elevator buttons as if they hold the secrets of the universe, and Amelia stares at the floor numbers ticking by with laser focus.

"What if she's asleep?" Charlotte whispers as we reach the second floor.

"It's four in the afternoon," I point out. "Trust me, she's not asleep."

"What if she thinks we don't want her?" Henry asks, his voice small. "What if she's crying?"

I ruffle Henry's hair. "Then we'll make sure she stops crying and knows exactly how much we love her."

The corridor seems to go on forever like the final leg of a marathon. Room 237 is at the far end. We approach the door as a unit, the children clustering around me like ducklings.

"Who's going to knock?" Charlotte whispers.

"I will, pet," I declare, taking a deep breath. "But you lot need to be ready with your apologies."

Henry tugs at my sleeve. "Can I go first? I practiced what I wanna say."

I give him a light squeeze. "You have first dibs, champ."

Now or never. I raise my hand and knock three times. Silence follows, then I hear the muffled sound of movement. The door opens a crack, and I catch a glimpse of Jennifer's face—her eyes red-rimmed and puffy, but still the most beautiful eyes I've ever seen.

"Fletcher?" Her voice catches, and her eyes flare wide. "What are you doing here?"

Before I can answer, Henry ducks under my arm and launches himself at her, wrapping his arms around her waist like a koala bear. "We're sorry! Please come home! I promise I won't wet the bed anymore!"

Josh tries to seem cool and collected as he steps forward. "What Henry means is that we want you to come back."

Jennifer's eyes widen when she sees the four children crowded in her doorway. Her gaze finally lands on me, a question in her eyes.

I give her a gentle smile. "May we come in, pet?"

She hesitates for a moment before nodding and stepping back. Henry remains attached to her waist. The room is standard hotel fare—beige everything and unremarkable, but Jennifer has somehow made it feel like home simply by being here.

"We had a family meeting," Amelia explains, stepping forward with the authority of someone twice her age. "And we decided you're an idiot for leaving."

"Amelia," I warn, but Jennifer's lips twitch upward slightly.

"She's right," Charlotte concurs, moving to Jennifer's other side. "We never said we didn't want you. We were just surprised about you and Dad."

I watch Jennifer's expression as she processes their words. The tears threatening to spill over make my throat tighten. Henry still hasn't let go of her, and honestly, I don't blame him.

"You came all the way here to tell me I'm an idiot?" Jennifer asks, her eyes faintly red but her voice calm.

"We came to bring you home," Josh announces matter-of-factly. "Where you belong."

My chest swells with pride at my son's simple declaration. But it's Jennifer's face that captures my attention—the way her expression crumbles with relief, the tears that finally spill over her cheeks.

"You really want me to come home?" she whispers, her voice breaking on the last word.

"Yes!" all four children shout in unison.

I move closer, gently extracting Henry from her so I can take Jennifer's hands in mine. "We had it all wrong, love. They weren't upset about us being together. They were scared you'd leave them like Claudia did."

Jennifer searches my face. "And now?"

"They've made it quite clear that I'm a complete pillock for letting you walk out that door," I say, earning giggles from the children. "They want you to stay—and so do I. This family wouldn't be whole without you, Jennifer."

She leaps into my arms.

Chapter Twenty

Jennifer

I fling my arms around Fletcher's neck while my feet dangle above the floor. I kiss every inch of his face while the kids grin and giggle. When I finally step back onto the floor, I'm crying and laughing at the same time. Fletcher pulls out a handkerchief to dab my eyes dry—and he doesn't even flinch when I blow my nose like a foghorn.

Fletcher seems baffled by my behavior, and I don't blame him. But his confusion swiftly melts into a sweet smile as he brushes his thumb across my cheek. "Hush, love, don't cry."

"They're happy tears. I know it's silly, but I just—I never expected this." My voice catches as I gaze at the children's faces, full of so such hope. "I thought I'd ruined everything, but you guys showed me how much I love this family and want to be a part of it."

Fletcher sets me down, clasping my hand as he turns toward the children. "I think it's time we all went home. Don't you?"

"Yes, definitely." *Home.* That word has never felt more right.

Henry claps and whoops. "Can we get ice cream on the way? To celebrate?"

"It's not even dinner time yet," Fletcher says, but his stern tone doesn't match the smile tugging at his lips.

"This is definitely an ice cream occasion," I counter, earning whoops from the kids. "I'll even treat everyone including the grandparents. I'll let them know by text."

"Why not caramel fudge ice cream cake instead?" Charlotte asks hopefully. "We could eat it at home."

"That sounds perfect," I agree. "But I suspect Henry will get ice cream cake all over his face."

The boy in question grins. "Yeah, I think so too."

As I gather my purse and the few things I had unpacked, Amelia approaches me hesitantly. She's hanging back from the others with her arms crossed in the protective stance I've come to recognize. "Please don't leave us again, Jennifer."

"Never, ever again." I give her a quick squeeze. "You have my word. It would take a tornado to tear me away from you guys."

Fletcher looks at me, though he speaks to the children. "Well, what are we waiting for? Ice cream cake awaits!"

As we drive toward the ice cream parlor, the kids all start singing a kid-friendly pop song. Even Josh gets into the fun. The ice cream shop is about to close by the time we get there, but the owner takes pity on us. He gives us a ready-made cake that looks absolutely scrumptious.

Once we're back at home, we enjoy our celebratory treat. The children don't make any messes at all, which seems like a miracle sent down straight from heaven. Now that they have full tummies, they all head for the rooms and crawl into bed, falling asleep quickly.

The grandparents returned to their homes.

Fletcher and I abscond to our room and fall asleep before we can even think about making love.

For the next five weeks, we take time to get used to the new dynamics of our family. It's wonderful.

Today, Fletcher makes pancakes for the whole family. The kitchen smells like butter and syrup, and the morning sunlight streams through the windows, turning everything golden. It's Saturday, which means no rushing around for school or work. Just us, together. Our little family.

"Careful with that batter," I warn as Henry tilts the mixing bowl at a dangerous angle. "Your dad will have a fit if we have to clean the ceiling again."

"That was one time," Fletcher protests, flipping a perfectly golden pancake with a dramatic flourish. "And it was your fault for suggesting we add food coloring."

"Red pancakes were cool," Josh says, not looking up from his book. Even at breakfast, that boy has his nose buried in something educational.

Fletcher leans forward with that sneaky glint in his eyes that means he's about to give the children a whopper of a tall tale. "Did I ever tell you lot about the time when I was just a boy and my paper airplane flew around the world twice? Before landing back in my hand with postcards from twelve different countries? Would you like to hear the story?"

The kids' lean forward, entranced by his wacky story.

I pour coffee into Fletcher's mug, letting my fingers brush against his while I hand it to him. Six weeks of being officially together, and my heart still does a little flip whenever we touch.

"Thanks, pet," he murmurs, his voice still morning-rough in a way that makes my toes curl.

Charlotte appears in the doorway, her hair a tangled mess. She rubs sleep from her eyes. "Are there chocolate chips in them?"

"Naturally," Fletcher answers, as if chocolate-less pancakes are an absurd concept. "What kind of tyrant do you think I am?"

Charlotte grins and slides onto her usual seat at the table. The domesticity of this moment gives me a lovely tingle. I can't believe how easily I've slipped into their lives, how normal it is to be standing here in pajama shorts and Fletcher's old t-shirt, helping serve breakfast to these children I adore.

"Where's Amelia?" I ask, noticing our eldest is missing.

Josh shrugs. "Probably still asleep. She was up late texting with her friends."

Amelia shuffles into the kitchens, rubbing her eyes and yawning.

Charlotte clucks her tongue. "Ooh, you're in big trouble, Amelia. No texting during or after dinner, remember?"

"That doesn't apply to me. I'm the oldest, so I get special perks."

Fletcher and I exchange a look, then he turns on his Big Daddy voice. "You know that isn't true, pet. *No texting before or after dinner.* If any of you lot disobey my command, your texting privileges will be revoked permanently."

Josh screws up his mouth. "Being a kid sucks."

"No bad language. Remember the rules." Fletcher squints at Josh. "No exceptions."

Becoming a parent so swiftly has been a whirlwind, and learning the ropes in my own new family is much harder than I expected. I catch Fletcher's eye again, and this time his expression softens. Being the disciplinarian while also trying to maintain the romantic connection between us is a delicate balance we're both still navigating.

Before I realize it, summer break has arrived.

Fletcher strolls over and drapes his arm casually around my shoulders. "So, what's the plan for this first day of summer break, then? Any brilliant ideas? You'll be alone with the children all day long while I'm at work."

"I thought the kids and I might go to the community pool," I suggest, pouring more orange juice for Henry who's already demolished his first glass. "It's supposed to hit ninety degrees today."

"Swimming!" Henry punches the air, accidentally knocking his fork onto the floor.

I bend to retrieve it, narrowly avoiding a collision with Fletcher who has the same idea. Our heads bump gently, and we both laugh. These little moments still feel like magic.

"Sorry, love," he murmurs, his fingers brushing mine as he hands me the fork.

"Swimming is sooo boring," Amelia declares, finally joining us at the table. Her hair is gathered into a messy bun, and she's wearing the oversized T-shirt she always sleeps in. "We should do something really based to celebrate not having to go to school."

"How about the pool at the rec center?" I suggest, pouring her a glass of orange juice. "It's cool. Literally."

"Ha-ha." She plays it cool, but I catch the hint of a smile. Amelia's been warming up to me more every day, our relationship strengthening like a tender seedling finally getting enough sunlight. "But the rec center is for old people like you and Dad."

"What would you recommend, then?" Fletcher asks, sliding a plate of pancakes in front of her.

He deftly ignored Amelia's old-people remark.

She shrugs, drowning her breakfast in syrup. "I dunno. Maybe the new adventure park? They have zip lines and stuff."

I think my eyes are literally bulging. "I don't think your father would like that."

The man I adore slides his arms around my waist from behind. "You are correct, love. High-speed, high-flying acrobatics are not on the menu."

Despite the children's disappointment, we all come up with some genuinely kid-friendly ideas for having fun today. We settle on two adventures—the Strategic Air Command & Aerospace Museum, and the Durham Museum. Both establishments offer plenty of hands-on fun.

By the time Fletcher leaves for work, the children are so excited that we head for our first destination right away, ordering breakfast through a drive-through window at a local fast-food joint.

Now it's time for today's adventure.

The Strategic Air Command & Aerospace Museum turns out to be a perfect choice. The kids race from exhibit to exhibit, their enthusiasm infectious as they explore everything from vintage aircraft to space capsules. I trail behind them, smiling as I watch Henry pretend to pilot a fighter jet while making elaborate whooshing sounds.

"Look, Jennifer!" Charlotte calls out from across the room. "This plane is older than you!"

"Thanks for that reminder," I call back, earning snickers from Josh who's studying a display about the history of flight with his usual intensity.

Even Amelia seems genuinely interested, though she tries to play it cool as she examines the cockpit of a restored bomber. I catch her taking a selfie when she thinks no one's looking.

"This is actually pretty awesome," she admits grudgingly when I join her.

After we've explored the rest of the exhibits, we drive to our next destination—the Durham Museum. It's a completely different experience from the aerospace museum. This converted train station offers a grandeur that immediately captures all of us. The soaring ceilings and restored art deco details make me feel like I've stepped back in time.

"Whoa," Josh breathes, his neck craned back to take in the massive chandelier. "This place is lit."

Keeping up with the slang of the younger generation gives me a headache. But fortunately, Josh tells me that "lit" means something is really good.

Henry immediately gravitates toward the working soda fountain. "Can we get ice cream? Please? I promise I won't ask for anything else today."

"You literally just had breakfast two hours ago," I remind him, but I'm already calculating whether we have time for a treat.

The museum's interactive exhibits prove to be just as engaging as the aircraft displays. Charlotte becomes fascinated with the old-fashioned general store, carefully examining every vintage product on the shelves. Amelia finds herself drawn to the fashion exhibit, though, the expression on her face tells me she's genuinely interested rather than just humoring me.

"These dresses are actually pretty cool," she admits, running her fingers lightly over a display case containing a flapper dress from the 1920s. "Can you imagine wearing something like this to school?"

"You'd certainly make an impression," I laugh, imagining Amelia's dramatic entrance to her high school hallway.

By the time we come home, the children are yawning and need a nap. Even Josh and Amelia are sleepy. I doze on the sofa, rousing only when I hear Fletcher's car coming up the drive. As the front door clicks shut, my eyes flutter open, and Fletcher leans over me for a kiss.

Oh yes, I love my life.

Chapter Twenty-One

Fletcher

After twelve days of working nonstop at the hotel, coming home only for dinner and sleep, I finally have a chance to decompress. Half my staff had been sick. The temps I hired needed more training than I'd hoped would be the case. Now, I'm lying in bed with Jennifer—and listening to her softly snoring. It's adorable.

In the morning, I hug my rug rats and then say goodbye to Jennifer. I'd love to kiss her, but I'm in a hurry. I slept in slightly too long, and now I must drive a touch faster than usual to avoid being late for work. Once I've gotten situated in my office and have my chair adjusted correctly, I bring out the piles of paperwork that have turned into a precarious mountain on my desk.

I've just picked up my pen when my mobile phone rings. I recognize the name of the caller instantly and pick up on the second ring. "Hello, Dominic. How is jolly old England today?"

"Bloody fantastic. But that's not why I rang you."

"You had more than time-zone discussions in mind, eh?"

"Time zones?" Dom chuckles. "No, Fletch. We have an invitation for you and your new love. The little monsters will enjoy it too."

I blow out a sigh. "Is there a point to this conversation? I am at work, you know."

"And as uptight as ever, eh?" Dom clucks his tongue. "I rang you because Florry and Patty are worried about you. Apparently, you've become severely uptight."

"Patty? How do you know my mother-in-law?"

"She and Florry have become good friends."

How in the world Dominic Rigby knows about my life here in Nebraska is beyond my comprehension. "Dom, I am very busy right now."

"And that's why we're coming to help you."

Coming to help me? Ohhh, I don't like the sound of that. "I'm far too busy to waste time entertaining you, Chelsea, and your two children here in America."

Dominic bursts into uproarious laughter. "No, no, Fletch. You've got it all wrong. It won't be just your family and ours." He lowers his voice to a stage whisper. "The American Wives Club is coming to your rescue, whether you like it or not."

I've heard of the American Wives Club—from Dominic. It's a group of busybody women who are determined to meddle in other people's lives. The Club did help Hugh Parrish and his American love, Avery, after a scandal nearly ruined Hugh. And I've heard that the Club was created when Scotsman Rory MacTaggart married American Emery on a whim. That worked out well, I believe.

But still…

"No, Dom, do not come to America to save me from…whatever."

"You misunderstand, mate. The game is already afoot."

I freeze, unable to speak for at least five seconds. "What does that mean, precisely?"

"You are the American Wives Club's latest mission. And since our mates are already flying to Nebraska on three private jets owned by three billionaires, you have no choice." Dominic chuckles darkly. "Give in, Mr. Murgatroyd, you can't escape the Club."

Bloody hell. I thought my life was already a sodding mess, but my old friend seems determined to cock it up even more.

"Still there, Fletch?"

"Ah, yes."

"Excellent. Now listen up." He pauses—for dramatic effect, I'm sure. Then he declares, "The first contingent will arrive tomorrow. Oh, and we've hired some people to help with the logistics."

"But the hotel—"

"Trust me. Everything has already been taken care of."

Dominic Rigby hangs up on me. *The bloody wanker.*

I stare at my phone as if it's morphed into a man-eating lion. The American Wives Club? Coming here? To Nebraska? To help me with what, exactly?

My hands shake slightly as I set the phone down. I've heard the stories about that so-called club—how they swoop in like well-meaning hurricanes, rearranging people's lives with the subtlety of a marching band. Sure, they helped Hugh. But his situation was different. Hugh, Lord Sommerleigh, needed saving from a scandal. I only need to get through my sodding paperwork.

I grab my mobile phone and dial Jennifer's number.

She answers on the third ring. "Fletcher? Are you okay? You just left twenty minutes ago."

"Jennifer, love, we have an outlandish situation to deal with." I rake my free hand through my hair, probably making it stand up at ridiculous angles. "Remember how I mentioned my friend Dominic from university? The one who married Chelsea, an American?"

"Vaguely, yes. Why?"

I draw in a deep breath and exhale it slowly. "Well, Dom just rang to inform me that the American Wives Club means to descend upon us like a horde of locusts. Tomorrow. In three private jets."

Silence on the other end. Then: "I'm sorry, what now?"

"Apparently, my mother and Patty have been conspiring with this…informal organization. They claim I need rescuing from my uptight ways." I slouch in my chair, staring at the ceiling tiles. "Dom says they're already on the way."

Jennifer's laughter bubbles through the phone, and I can almost picture the woman I love shaking her head. "Fletcher, only you would make it sound like we're being invaded by giant robots. It's probably nothing more than some friends wanting to visit."

"*You don't understand.*" My emphatic tone might have been overkill. I speak softly even though my office door is closed. "These people are notorious. They call themselves a 'club,' but they're more like a special ops team for romantic interventions. They've been responsible for at least a dozen high-profile matchmakings and relationship rescues. Or so Dominic told me a few years ago."

"And they're coming here? For us?" Jennifer sounds more intrigued than alarmed, which worries me further.

"Isn't that what I said? *Yes, three private jets full of meddling socialites and their equally meddling husbands.*" I massage my temple where a headache is already forming. "And according to Dom, they've 'handled' my work situation. Whatever that means."

I hear Jennifer moving about, probably pacing as she does when she's thinking. "Well, we should at least meet them before you start panicking. Maybe they're just friendly people."

"Friendly people call ahead. They don't commandeer private jets and rearrange my work schedule."

"You're probably right," I concede, though my gut tells me otherwise. "But how do I explain this to tell the children? 'Oh, by the way, a group of American socialites is coming to reorganize our lives because your grandmothers think I'm too stressed?"

"We'll figure it out together," Jennifer assures me. "Sweetie, whatever happens, we'll handle it. You, me, and the kids. That's what families do."

The word 'family,' spoken in Jennifer's sweet voice, settles my anxiety just enough that I no longer worry I might have a coronary. "You are right as always, love."

"I should probably warn you—I'm dying to meet these mysterious club members."

"Sounds like an epic disaster to me," I mutter. Then I glance at my paperwork mountain, wondering if any of it will matter once the American Wives Club descends upon us. I shut my eyes and groan pathetically. I can already tell Jennifer's too curious for her own good. "I should go, I suppose. According to Dom, I have about twenty-four hours to prepare for an invasion. I'd better say goodbye now."

"Love you, sweetie."

"I love you too, Jennifer." And I need to marry that woman soon. But my friends seem determined to take over my life, at least for a few days.

As I hang up the phone, I stare at my desk and wonder how I'm supposed to concentrate knowing what's coming. A knock at my door interrupts my spiraling thoughts.

"Come in," I call out, expecting Marjorie with the morning reports.

Instead, my assistant manager, Debbie, enters. She looks suspiciously cheerful. "Morning, boss! I've got some interesting news."

"Let me guess—you've been contacted by someone from the American Wives Club?"

Debbie's eyes bulge. "How did you know? A woman called Emery MacTaggart contacted me this morning. Said she was handling some logistics for your friends."

Wonderful. Someone I've never met and had never heard of until this morning wants to arrange my life.

I sink into my chair as if quicksand might swallow me up. "And what exactly did this Emery person say?"

"She was super nice, actually. Totally professional too." Debbie sits down across from my desk. "She's arranged for additional temporary staff to cover your duties for the next week. Said you'd be needing time for 'family matters.'"

My eye twitches. Am I developing a tic? "Family matters? I assume that means *my* family."

"Uh-huh. That's what she told me. Oh, and she's booked the entire east wing of the hotel for their group. They'll need conference rooms, catering facilities, and something called a 'war room.'"

A war room? *Crikey.* I sink deeper into my chair. "Debbie, please tell me you didn't agree to any of this."

"Well, she did mention that payment would be handled in full, plus a substantial bonus for any inconvenience." Debbie smiles sheepishly. "It seemed rude to refuse such a generous offer."

Of course it did. Money talks, and clearly, the American Wives Club speaks fluent currency.

"How substantial are we talking?" I ask, though I'm not sure I want to know.

"Let's just say it's enough to cover your salary for the next six months." Debbie's smile widens. "Emery also mentioned upgrading our conference facilities. Permanently. As a gift."

I gawp at her, speechless. These people operate on a level I can't even comprehend. Who casually throws around six-figure sums to rearrange a stranger's work schedule?

"All right, then." I stand up, tugging my suit jacket down. "Get back to your duties, please, Debbie."

As she leaves the room, my skin begins to itch. Whatever I'm being roped into, I suspect it will be a circus of monumental proportions.

Chapter Twenty-Two

Jennifer

You need to explain that to me again, Fletcher." I'm lying in bed next to the man I love, but nothing he's told me in the last ten minutes makes any sense. He might as well be talking Swahili. "Are you saying only American women are allowed at this bizarre event? That can't be what you meant, but you need to explain the situation a little better. My head is swimming."

His lips quirk into a lopsided smile. "I felt the same way when Dominic laid out the Club's plans."

"So, the 'club' really is just for Americans?"

"No, no, not only American women," Fletcher explains, running his hand through his already-mussed hair. "The American Wives Club began with American women who married Scottish men, but now it includes British couples too."

I prop myself up on one elbow and study his face. The worry lines around his eyes have deepened since yesterday. "So, these people—these strangers—are flying in on three private jets to…do what exactly? Reorganize our lives? Plan our wedding? Start a reality TV show?"

Fletcher lets out a bark of laughter that sounds more stressed than amused. "Honestly? I'm not entirely sure. Dominic was maddeningly vague about their actual intentions." He rolls onto his side to face me properly. "All I know is that my mother and Patty apparently reached out to them because they think I'm too 'uptight' and need intervention."

"Your mother thinks you need a romantic intervention?" I just manage to smother a snort of laugh. "Fletcher, we're already together. We're happy. What more do they want?"

"That's exactly what I'd like to know." He shuts his eyes and groans. "But with this group's reputation, they must have some elaborate scheme brewing. Marriage proposals involving flash mobs, or surprise wedding ceremonies, or God knows what else."

I sit up, staring down at him. "Wait. Marriage proposals? Is that something you've been thinking about?"

Fletcher makes a sheepish face and looks away. "Well, ah, I mean…would that be such a terrible thing? We might have known each other for a relatively brief time, but I already know I love you and want to spend the rest of my life with you. It's too soon, though, I guess. I took it slow with Claudia and look how that turned out."

"Oh, sweetie, you know I'd never treat you the way she did."

"I do know that. You've changed my life, and I'm so happy you did." He sits up, turning toward me. "Will you marry me, Jennifer?"

"Are you serious?"

"Dead serious."

Joy sweeps over me, and I burst into a fit of giggling. "Yes, Fletcher, I would love to marry you. Tonight, tomorrow, whenever or wherever. As soon as possible wouldn't be soon enough."

"Brilliant!" He drags me into his arms and kisses me with so much passion that it takes my breath away.

When our lips finally part, I can barely breathe. "The kids will be thrilled. Amelia and Charlotte have been hinting that we should tie the knot. The boys will love it too, I'm sure."

"We should let the children know first thing in the morning."

And we wind up doing just that.

The next morning, I'm practically bursting with excitement, like a kid on Christmas morning. I wake up before Fletcher's alarm goes off, my mind already racing with thoughts of telling the children. Fletcher stirs beside me, his arm tightening around my waist.

"Morning," he mumbles against my hair. "Ready for the big announcement?"

"I couldn't be more ready." I kiss his stubbled cheek. "Though I'm slightly terrified of the American Wives invasion that's coming."

Fletcher groans. "Don't remind me. Let's focus on one potential disaster at a time."

We wait until everyone's seated for breakfast. Fletcher makes his famous waffles while I set the table, our eyes meeting across the kitchen in secret glances that make my heart flutter like I'm sixteen again. Henry notices, of course.

"Why are you two being so weird?" he asks, syrup dripping from his chin.

"Sweetie, we're not being weird," I protest, though I can feel my cheeks heating up. "We're happy, that's all."

"You're always happy," Charlotte points out, not looking up from her perfectly arranged waffle stack. "This is different. Like, secret happy."

Across the table, he raises a single brow at me, and I smile with my lips sealed. Time to dive in.

Fletcher claps his fork down. "Listen up, you little monsters. Jennifer and I do have something to tell you all."

The reaction is immediate. Josh stops mid-chew. Amelia's head snaps up from her phone. Charlotte bounces in her seat like she's been electrified.

"Are you getting married?" she shrieks before we can say another word.

My jaw drops. "How did you—"

"I KNEW IT!" Henry jumps up and starts doing some sort of victory dance around the table, his arms flailing like he's conducting an invisible orchestra. "Jennifer's going to be our real mom now!"

The way he calls me his "real mom" with such pure joy melts my heart.

"Wait, hold on," Amelia says, but she's grinning. "You two are actually getting married? Like, for real?"

"Yes, pet, for real," Fletcher confirms, reaching across the table to squeeze my hand. "I asked Jennifer last night, and she said yes."

Josh sets down his fork. "When's the wedding? How many people will be there? Do we get to help plan it?"

Charlotte gawps at me. "Will Jennifer adopt us?"

Fletcher chuckles. "Slow down, love. We literally just decided twelve hours ago. But I doubt adoption is necessary."

Charlotte hops up and down in her chair so enthusiastically that I'm worried she's going to launch herself into orbit. "What kind of dress will you wear? Can I be the maid of honor? Will there be dancing?"

"Breathe, Charlotte," I laugh, my own excitement bubbling over. "We haven't planned any of those details yet."

"But you will, right?" Amelia asks, and there's something vulnerable in her voice that I've never heard before. "You'll let us help plan everything?"

"Yes, absolutely we will," Fletcher says firmly. "This wedding is about becoming a proper family."

Henry stops his victory dance and starts waving his arms around. "This is the best day ever! Even better than when we went to the water park!"

I hug him back, breathing in his syrup-scented hair. "I love you too, sweetheart."

"Group hug!" Charlotte declares, and suddenly all four children are piling on top of me, their arms tangling in a chaotic embrace that nearly knocks me off my chair.

"Careful," Fletcher laughs, steadying my chair before I topple backward. "Let's not break Jennifer before the wedding, shall we?"

I'm laughing so hard I can barely breathe, surrounded by these four amazing children who have somehow become mine. When I finally extract myself from the pile of Murgatroyd offspring, I notice Fletcher watching us with tender expression.

"So, when are we telling the grandparents?" Josh asks, returning to his breakfast with newfound enthusiasm.

Fletcher and I exchange glances.

"Actually," he begins, "they might already know. In fact, they may have orchestrated quite the celebration already."

Amelia's eyes narrow. "What do you mean?"

"Well, that's where things get a bit complicated."

Charlotte's brows furrow. "Complicated? In what way?"

I hesitate and I try to figure out how to explain the American Wives Club without sounding completely unhinged. "Your grandmothers seem to have contacted some, uh…friends to help us celebrate. But those friends won't arrive until after the wedding. Right, Fletcher?"

"That's right."

Amelia scrunches her lips, her tone suspicious. "What sort of friends, Dad? The adult kind or the kid kind?"

Fletcher shrugs. "A bit of both. A group called the American Wives Club will be coming to Millbrook Valley. They're, ah, a bit enthusiastic about helping couples in whatever way they deem necessary."

"Like matchmakers?" Josh asks, his forehead wrinkling.

"Sort of," I hedge. "Except we're already matched, so they're more like…celebration planners? On steroids?"

Henry's eyes go wide. "Are they famous?"

"No, sweetie, they're not celebrities," I assure him. "They're very, very determined people who like to help couples, that's all. Some of them are very wealthy too. Oh, and Lord Sommerleigh is a viscount."

Charlotte gasps. "Is that like the royal family?"

"No, Hugh isn't royal, though he is a member of the House of Lords," Fletcher explains. "And they're not exactly famous in the traditional sense. Influential is a better word. My mate Dominic Rigby is a former cricket champion."

Henry grins. "I love crickets! They make a really cool sound."

"Not that sort of cricket, Henry." I ruffle his hair. "Dominic isn't an insect. He played the sport called cricket, though now he's retired."

I squeeze Fletcher's hand, and the tension in his fingers releases a touch. "What your father means is that these people are known for helping couples celebrate their relationships in very…creative ways."

"They're party planners?" Josh asks skeptically.

"Much more than that," Fletcher says. "They're more like a romantic SWAT team."

I almost choke on my coffee at his description. "Fletcher!"

"What? It's true." He turns to the children with a sigh. "Look, these people mean well, but they tend to go overboard. Very, very overboard. With everything."

Maybe I should feel anxious about everything he's told us, but instead, I can't wait to meet his friends.

Chapter Twenty-Three

Fletcher

What two mothers and four children can do in three days astounds me. Mum and Patty took over the wedding details, which mostly involved helping Jennifer find her dream gown. Amelia and Charlotte dived into dress shopping with gusto for their bridesmaid ensembles. While the ladies handled that portion of the big event, Dad and Bob assisted me in finding the right suit. Henry and Josh needed suits as well since they will be my junior groomsmen.

The big day has arrived at last.

Are those real butterflies flitting around in my belly? No, that's barmy. What a daft thing to suggest, even in my own mind. I wasn't nervous at all when I married Claudia, but I reckon that's because she wasn't the right woman for me. She gave me four wonderful children who, despite being a large handful, became my world. I would never abandon them the way Claudia had done, and I know Jennifer wouldn't do that either.

Now that I'm standing at the altar, I experience a touch of anxiety. But it's the good sort of butterflies. I glance around at my junior groomsmen. Josh keeps adjusting his bowtie while Henry behaves as if he has genuine ants in his pants. They both stand up straight, seeming almost regal in their suits. Henry hasn't done anything inappropriate, such as bringing his favorite worm into the chapel. I'm grateful for that.

My father and Bob are seated in the front row with Mum and Patty. Several of my employees from the hotel are here, looking smart. Jennifer's parents are here too. They flew in from Arkansas yesterday morning, looking both proud and slightly overwhelmed by the chaos that surrounds every Murgatroyd family gathering. Jennifer's mum keeps dabbing at her eyes with a lace handkerchief, while her father sits ramrod straight, clearly trying not to let his emotions show.

The chapel doors open.

Charlotte emerges first, looking as lovely as an angel in her pale pink bridesmaid dress. She's carrying a small bouquet with the solemnity of someone handling the Crown Jewels, though I catch her grinning at Henry.

Next comes Amelia, and my heart swells to see how poised and pretty my eldest daughter looks. I'm grateful to see her genuinely happy. I haven't seen that since before her mother left. She's wearing the same shade of pink as Charlotte but somehow manages to seem both elegant and age-appropriate at the same time.

The music swells just as Jennifer appears in the doorway.

My throat thickens, and I forget how to breathe properly.

She's beyond stunning. Her dress is simple but elegant—ivory silk that flows like water, with delicate lace sleeves that make her look like a princess from a fairy tale. But it's her smile that undoes me completely. She's gazing directly at me with so much love and joy that I get choked up.

Her father walks beside her, his arm linked through hers, but I can barely focus on anything except Jennifer's face. She glows with happiness, her green eyes sparkling with unshed tears of joy.

As they approach the altar, I catch a glimpse of Henry fidgeting beside me. He's trying to wave at Jennifer while maintaining his serious junior groomsman pose, and the sight makes me grin despite my nerves. When Jennifer reaches me, her father gives her hand a gentle squeeze before placing it in mine.

"You are..." The words catch in my throat. "Absolutely breathtaking."

Jennifer's eyes crinkle at the corners as she smiles. "You clean up rather nicely yourself, Mr. Murgatroyd."

The minister clears his throat, bringing us back to the moment. I reluctantly tear my gaze away from Jennifer to face forward, though I keep her hand firmly in mine. I can't bear to let go, even for a moment.

"Dearly beloved," the minister begins, his voice carrying through the small chapel.

I try to listen to his words, but my mind keeps drifting to the woman beside me. How did I get so lucky? Before Jennifer, I was drowning in single parenthood, convinced I'd never find someone who could love not only me but my barmy brood as well. And now here's Jennifer, promising to be my wife, my partner in all the ups and downs of life.

"Fletcher," the minister prompts gently, and I realize he's been waiting for me to recite my vows.

I clear my throat, lifting my chin slightly. "I, Fletcher Ralph Murgatroyd, take you, Jennifer Marie Cordell, to be my lawfully wedded wife."

The traditional words seems inadequate for everything I must say to her. I want to promise that I'll never take for granted the way she makes Henry's lunch with dinosaur-shaped sandwiches, or how she patiently helps Josh with his science projects, or the way she's broken through Amelia's walls with gentle persistence.

Instead, I stick to the script. But I pour every ounce of love I feel for her into those simple words. Jennifer's voice is steady and clear when she repeats her vows back to me. Her fingers tremble slightly in mine, but her eyes never leave my face. "I, Jennifer Marie Cordell, take you, Fletcher Ralph Murgatroyd, to be my lawfully wedded husband."

"Do you have the rings?" the minister asks.

Josh hurries forward. He presents the small velvet box with both hands, his demeanor somber.

I take Jennifer's ring from the box and slide it onto her finger. Her smile grows even brighter, if that's possible, and I watch as tears finally trickle down her cheeks.

"With this ring," I say, my voice stronger now, "I thee wed."

Jennifer's hands shake as she places my ring on my finger. The simple gold band holds within it the weight of promises--of forever. I will never let this woman go. "With this ring, I thee wed."

"By the power vested in me," the minister says, "I now pronounce you husband and wife. You may kiss the bride."

I don't need to be told twice. I cup Jennifer's face in my hands and kiss her with everything I have. The chapel erupts in cheers and applause, but all I can hear is the thundering of my own heart and the cheers from the pews.

"We did it," Jennifer whispers in my ear.

"Yes, we bloody well did." I grin and kiss her again, with no less intensity than the first time.

"Congratulations, Mr. and Mrs. Murgatroyd!" Henry shouts, abandoning all pretense of junior groomsman dignity and launching himself at us both.

I laugh and scoop him up with one arm while keeping my other around Jennifer. *My wife.* The word sends a thrill through me that I wasn't expecting.

"Did you see me wave?" Henry asks. "I tried to be sneaky about it."

"You were very sneaky indeed," Jennifer assures him, pressing a kiss to his forehead that leaves a faint lipstick mark.

Charlotte and Amelia join us at the altar, and suddenly we're surrounded by a tangle of arms and excited chatter. Over their heads, I catch sight of my parents beaming from the front row. Dad wipes at his eyes covertly, while Mum clutches her handkerchief and dabs at her eyes.

While the guests make their way out of the chapel and into the adjacent dining hall, which has become the reception venue. The mothers and my daughters conspired to turn a drab hall into a stunningly romantic place.

Jennifer and I share our first dance as husband and wife. More cheers accompany us, especially from the mothers and my daughters.

Once we've had enough of the party, we're escorted into a limo that takes us directly to the small airport situated just outside of town. I had arranged for us to enjoy our honeymoon at a lovely little resort nestled among rolling hills. We had both agreed the honeymoon would be one-night only.

The bellboy has just left the room, and the soft click of the latch means one thing. It's time to ravish my wife.

I stride toward Jennifer, *my wife*, as my pulse accelerates. She's standing by the window, bathed in the soft glow of sunset that paints her skin golden. The wedding dress still hugs her curves perfectly, and I can't wait to peel it off her.

"Hello, Mrs. Murgatroyd," I purr, wrapping my arms around her waist from behind.

She leans back against me, her body pliant and warm. "I love the sound of that."

I press my lips to the curve of her neck, breathing in her scent—vanilla and something uniquely Jennifer. My hands slide around her waist, pulling her flush against me so she can feel exactly what she does to me.

"I've been wanting to get you alone all day," I growl against her ear. "Devouring you is all the food I need."

Jennifer wriggles against me in my arms, cupping my groin with one hand. "Then what are you waiting, Mr. Murgatroyd? Fuck me like a madman."

I groan again, then pounce on her.

Chapter Twenty-Four

Jennifer

The look on Fletcher's face matches the feral growls that spill from his lips, and they make me so damn horny. But when Fletcher reaches for the zipper of my dress, his fingers fumble with the delicate fabric. I can feel his restraint cracking, the careful control he's maintained all day finally giving way to raw need.

"You have no idea what you've done to me, Jennifer. Standing there in that wedding dress, looking like an angel. But the beast in me needs to fuck you right now."

"Oh yes, I want that too. My cream is already dribbling down my thighs." As I help him with his zipper, the whisper of fabric against skin is the only sound in our honeymoon suite. The dress pools at my feet, leaving me in nothing but my shoes.

Fletcher's eyes darken as he drinks me in. "Christ, Jennifer. You're an angel with a dirty mind, and I love that."

With his hands, he maps every curve and hollow of my body, like he's memorizing me all over again. When his mouth follows the path his fingers traced, I arch beneath him. I can't help myself from moaning and even whimpering, especially when I glance down to see his dick fully erect with a drop of moisture poised on the head. Only Fletcher could reduce me to a puddle of molten lust. Every touch of his lips against my skin sets off a cascade of heated shivers. His hands are everywhere at once, reverent but hungry.

"I need you inside me," I gasp, tugging at his suit jacket. "Too many clothes."

Fletcher grins wickedly, shrugging off his jacket before loosening his tie with tantalizing slowness. I reach for his buttons, impatient to have him inside me, but he catches my wrists. "Let me take it slow, pet. I want to savor this moment."

"We have our whole lives for savoring. Make me scream now."

He unbuttons his shirt slowly, deliberately, one button at a time without ever breaking eye contact. It's the most erotic striptease I've ever witnessed, and I'm virtually quivering with need. When he finally stands before me in nothing but his boxer briefs, I can't speak because my chest is heaving. With my fingertips, I trace the hard planes of his chest and the defined muscles of his abdomen. The strength in his body never fails to thrill me.

"You're still wearing too much," Fletcher growls. "Get rid of the shoes."

I reach for him, but he has other ideas. Fletcher drops to his knees before me, placing wet kisses along my stomach and coiling his tongue inside my navel. His delicate licks drive me half out of my mind.

"Steady, love," he purrs.

"Fletcher, please," I gasp. "Oh God, please use your tongue on my clit and make me come."

He settles between my thighs. "My pleasure, Mrs. Murgatroyd."

The first touch of his tongue against my most sensitive region makes me cry out. I push my hands into his hair, holding him to me. He's merciless in the best way, alternating between gentle flicks and firm strokes that have me trembling within seconds.

"Yes, Fletcher, don't stop."

He grips my thighs with both hands, anchoring me as I begin to unravel from the sheer ecstasy. Every nerve ending is on fire, every touch magnified by the intimacy of our wedding night.

"Come for me, love," he murmurs against my skin. "Let me watch you melt for me."

"Yes, please, yes." I can see his dick has grown swollen and stiff, the head glistening with pre-cum, yet he still takes his time with me. But I can't stand the suspense anymore. "Push me over the edge, Fletcher. Can't stand the delicious torment anymore. My heart's beating so fast I..."

"No worries, love." He waddles closer until his face lies directly over my groin.

I grip his shoulders as he positions himself perfectly. The anticipation is almost unbearable—every cell in my body crying out for release. When his tongue finally makes contact with my swollen clit, I arch and nearly fall backward onto the bed. His strong hands anchor me.

"Fletcher!" His name is torn from my throat. "I'm about to—"

I can't speak anymore, can barely breathe.

My husband begins to scrape his tongue over my nub, devouring me as if my cream is the only sustenance he needs. I tangle my fingers in his dark hair, holding him against me as waves of pleasure build higher and higher. The man knows exactly how to drive me wild. The orgasm crashes over me like a tidal wave, my body bowing forward as pleasure rockets through me so powerfully that I lose my breath. My fingers are knotted in his silky locks.

Fletcher doesn't stop until I'm gasping, ruined by the devastating climax. Only then does he rise, his lips glistening, eyes dark with satisfaction and his own voracious need.

"My turn," I breathe, waving for him to back away. "Need more room for what I'm going to do to you. Been staring at your dick, and that bead of moisture on the head, since I first noticed it. Now I get to make you unravel—with my tongue."

But he shakes his head. "If you do that, I'll blow apart the instant your tongue touches the head of my cock."

"Don't worry. I won't let you explode until you're inside me." I move closer and kneel before his glorious dick. It waves in my face, and I can't resist licking my lips. "Now, for the pièce de résistance."

His chest is heaving now, like mine had done a moment ago. "Jennifer..."

I clasp his dick, leaning forward until my lips are only a few millimeters from his flesh. With the first lick, I have him hissing in a sharp breath. Then I coil my tongue around his flesh, again and again, while his eyes roll back in his head. His breaths have mutated into sharp, animalistic sounds. Just when he seems about to erupt, I pull away.

Fletcher grits his teeth. "You can't leave me like this, you vixen."

Grinning, I flop onto the bed backwards. "So come and get me."

He takes a flying leap, landing on the mattress on all fours.

Laughter bubbles out of me. "That was impressive. I never realized you're an acrobat."

"Only for you." He winks. "And only in the bedroom."

I wrap my legs around his waist, drawing him closer. "Take me, Fletcher. Make me yours and brand me with that gorgeous dick."

Fletcher plunges inside me with one smooth thrust, then he begins pounding into me with his cock, driving himself as deep inside me as possible, so deep in fact, that I swear I can feel his dick hitting the innermost wall of my channel. The intensity of the pleasure makes me quiver and beg for release. The bed creaks and thumps, but for once, he can fuck me wildly and unleash all his hunger for me no matter how much I scream. This is the most mind-blowing sexual experience of my life, and I never want it to stop.

But the tension in Fletcher's face tells me he needs to let go. He throws his head back and shouts as he explodes inside me, his release flooding through me while I shatter beneath him too. Our cries mingle through our honeymoon suite, and our bodies both tremble from the power of our lovemaking.

At last, we collapse together. The delicious weight of him settles on top of me, and I can't stop touching him. I trace patterns on his sweat-slicked back with my fingertips.

This man is my husband. *Mine.* And unlike Claudia, I will never run away from Fletcher.

"I love you so much," I whisper against his neck.

He rolls onto his side again, tugging me with him so we're face to face, our legs still tangled. His gaze is softer now, the wild hunger replaced by tenderness.

"I adore you too, darling." He says my new name as if it's precious—almost sacred. But then he smiles with wry humor. "You're saddled with my surname now. Sure you don't want to keep your maiden name?"

"Positive. I've waited a long time to meet my soulmate. Don't care how big a mouthful that surname is." I push up onto my elbow so I can look at the face of my beautiful husband. "Tomorrow, we go home and get back to normal life."

"Then we'd better fuck all night long, eh?"

I salute. "Yes, sir, we'd better."

We make love until after midnight, reveling in the freedom to do whatever we want, whenever we want—at least for one night. In the morning, we enjoy a sumptuous breakfast in the hotel's elegant dining room. The perfectly prepared eggs Benedict should make kick my appetite into high gear. But Fletcher keeps giving me smoldering looks across the table that distract me.

"Stop that," I hiss, my cheeks growing warm as he deliberately licks honey from his spoon in in an almost obscene manner.

He lifts one brow. "Stop what, Mrs. Murgatroyd?"

I love how he keeps using my new name like he's testing how it sounds. "You know exactly what you're doing." I shift in my chair, still deliciously sore from our marathon night of lovemaking. "We have to drive home and face the children in an hour."

"Plenty of time for one more—"

"No, no, no." I wag a finger at my husband, cutting him off before he can finish that thought. "We'll be late, and Henry will have convinced himself we've been kidnapped by pirates."

Fletcher chuckles, reaching across the table to clasp my hand. "Fair point. Though I quite like the idea of being kidnapped by you for another few hours."

"Behave yourself," I say, though I'm grinning as I squeeze his fingers. "Besides, I'm actually excited to get home and tell everyone about our perfect honeymoon night."

"Are you now?" His eyebrow arches. "And exactly how much detail are you planning to share with my children?"

I nearly choke on my orange juice. "Fletcher Ralph Murgatroyd! I meant telling them we had a wonderful time, not—" I lower my voice to a whisper. "Not about how you made me scream your name three times."

His grin turns sinfully hot. "Only three times? I was counting four, but maybe I lost track during that bit where you—"

"Shush, Fletcher," I hiss, though my body's already reacting to his teasing. "We need to be responsible adults, remember?"

"Responsible adults who just happen to be madly in love."

"And who have four children waiting for them at home." I narrow my gaze and pucker my lips, trying to sound forceful, but I fail. The smile spreading across my face doesn't help matters. "Save that look for tonight, after the kids are asleep."

He sighs dramatically, but the smile playing at the corners of his lips gives him away. "Fine. But I'm holding you to that promise."

After breakfast, we pack our overnight bags and head to the car. The drive home is filled with comfortable silence and occasional bursts of conversation about what awaits us. Four very excited children, that's for sure. I hope the grandparents weren't totally wiped out. The moment our car pulls up in the driveway, all the kids pour out of the house to attack us with joyful hugs.

This is my life these days—and I love it.

Chapter Twenty-Five

Doomsday has arrived on the outskirts of Millbrook Valley in the form of a baseball field. I feel as if a horde of Mongol warriors and their children have invaded my quiet life in Millbrook Valley, Nebraska. Well, my children are always a handful. But now, we must wrangle our own kids as well as those belonging to my friends. Perhaps calling this week doomsday is an act of outrageous hyperbole.

But no, it really is not.

Now, however, we must deal with the impending cricket match.

I haven't played the game in years, yet I allowed Dominic to coax me into participating. I hold Jennifer's hand while we approach the well-meaning contingent of Brits, Americans, and Scots who have traveled a long way to "help" me.

Emery MacTaggart, the ringleader of the American Wives Club, approaches us.

She offers us a dazzling smile and open arms—literally. She hugs us, then kisses our cheeks. Emery moves with the confidence of someone who seems like she must regularly command board-rooms.

But Dominic had confirmed Emery is not a tycoon. She spends most days wrangling her twin children.

"Fletcher Murgatroyd! Finally!" Emery hugs me like we're old friends rather than complete strangers. "Your mother has told us so much about you!"

I awkwardly pat her back, shooting Jennifer a desperate glance. My wife—god, I love calling her that—simply grins and mouths "be nice" at me.

"Lovely to meet you," I say. "Though I'm still not entirely clear on why you've all flown halfway around the world to...help me?"

Emery waves my question away with a slight laugh. "Your mother was worried. She told me you've been working yourself half to death, barely taking time to enjoy your beautiful family."

That's not quite accurate. But I don't get the chance to set the record straight.

Emery clasps her hands under her chin and starts talking again. "When we heard about the wedding, well, we just had to come celebrate with you guys."

Behind her, I spot a small army of couples and children milling about on the baseball field that's usually reserved for high-school events. I see Dominic with his wife Chelsea and their two children, looking thoroughly amused by my obvious discomfort. I see a tall man with light-brown hair who must be one of the Scots. He keeps his arm around a petite blonde woman while their children chase mine around the field.

"This is Rory MacTaggart, my husband," Emery explains, dragging her husband toward us. This is the man I'd pegged as a Scot earlier. "And that's Keely with the dark hair talking to your Amelia. Keely's American too and married to Evan MacTaggart, a Scottish billionaire."

My head spins while I attempt to keep track of everyone. There are dozens more adults heading this way, but at least everyone's children have gone to the playground on the other side of the green. I won't need to recall their names—not yet, anyway. For the next fifteen minutes, my brain is tested to its limits while I attempt to recall the names of every wife and husband pairing.

Emery helpfully goes on stating their names and even their occupations. "You've met my husband. But now let me introduce you to the other MacTaggarts—the ones who could come to this shindig, that is. MacTaggarts are very, um...prolific. Over there are Iain and his wife Rae along with their grown daughter, Malina, who came back from Scotland to join the festivities. She's American, like her mom. They brought their five-year-old son too."

Bloody hell, all these names. I think I'm getting a migraine, though I've never had one before.

Emery won't give up, though. She drags me and Jennifer round and round the green, and I learn even more names, such as Damian and Heidi Petrescu. He's a fortune teller, allegedly, and insists on telling me my fortune. He's clearing having me on.

Damian sandwiches his palms around mine.

He's making me slightly uncomfortable.

"You will find great joy on the cricket pitch tomorrow," Damian intones, his American accent mutating into…Romanian, I assume. Then he closes his eyes. "But beware the man in the red cap."

I extract my hands from his grip, trying not to appear rude. "Brilliant, thank you. I'll keep an eye out for suspicious headwear."

Jennifer muffles a laugh, squeezing my arm in silent support.

Damian releases my hands and grins, winking at me. "Don't worry, Fletcher. The only one here who can see the future is Kirsty."

"Is that a woman or a man?"

"Kirsty MacTaggart is a woman. Sorry, I meant Kirsty Turner. She's a lovely Scots lass who has *da-shealladh*, the second sight."

Yes, of course she does. Are these people having me on? Or are they all off their rockers?

"Fascinating," I mutter, desperately scanning for an escape route.

Thankfully, Jennifer jumps in. "We should probably check on the children. Henry tends to climb things when unsupervised."

A sigh of relief rushes out of me.

Just as we start walking toward the makeshift cricket pitch, Dominic jogs up to me. "We're having a practice match, and I figured you'd want to be there for that. I assume you are, ah, a bit rusty."

I must've made a sour face because Dom slaps me on the shoulder. "Try to get into the spirit, Fletch, eh?"

Jennifer kisses my cheek. "Go. Have a good time with your friends. I should hunt the kids down before they decide to boost a car and drive themselves to the water park."

"That's a wise decision."

I watch as my wife vanishes into the crowd.

Dominic claps a hand down on my shoulder. "I gather you're experiencing a small bout of nerves. Forget that bollocks, Fletch. Thane Buchanan brought plenty of his whisky from his distillery in Scotland. We have six cases of Thane Black Label, his signature whisky, as well as two cases of Sensual Secret and two of Dùndubhan Masterpiece."

"Duh-what? I don't need booze, Dom."

"Au contraire." He chuckles. "No one needs whisky more than you do right now."

Dominic drags me over to the edge of the pitch, where I now see the cases of whisky he mentioned.

An American man trots up to us, holding out his hand to shake. "I'm Derek Hahn. My wife is Diana Hahn, though you might know her better as Diana Sangster. She married me a while back."

Yes, that explains everything.

Derek grips my shoulder hard enough to make me wince. "Let's get you in the mood for a brief match. That'll get your blood pumping."

Though I don't need any "pumping," I might as well give in. My friends believe this will help me somehow, but I have my doubts. I stare at Derek, then at the cases of whisky, then back at Derek. "A brief match? How brief are we talking?"

"Just a quick knock-about," Dominic says, already rolling up his sleeves. "It'll get the blood flowing and remind your muscles what cricket is like."

He hands me a whisky bottle, urging me to drink.

Oh, why not. I open the bottle of Sensual Secret and down two big gulps. I wind up coughing. But quickly, my hacking dissipates, and the warm, smoky liquid infiltrates my senses.

"Damn, that's smooth," I rasp, my throat still burning pleasantly. The smoky flavor coats my tongue and warms my chest. Not bad whisky at all.

"Told you," Dominic grins, taking the bottle and having a swig himself. "Thane knows his spirits. And speaking of spirits, yours needs lifting, mate."

He waves toward a blond man who rushes over to us. Dom introduces him. "This is Chance Dixon. His brothers Dane and Reese are here too."

Someone across the green waves emphatically, dashing toward me and Dom. I squint across the green, trying to identify the rapidly approaching figure. The whisky has already made my vision slightly fuzzy around the edges. Drinking probably wasn't the wisest thing to do before attempting to play cricket for the first time in years.

Reese grins and extends his hand. "Fletcher! Heard you're a bit rusty on the pitch. Don't worry, we'll go easy on you."

"How reassuring." I shake his hand as the whisky burns pleasantly in my stomach, and I'm starting to understand why Dom thought alcohol might help. My nerves are definitely settling.

Dominic grins again. "Let's get you kitted out properly."

Within minutes, I'm ready to go in terms of my kit. As for playing the game…

Another man, who I don't recognize, dashes up to me. He slaps my arm—hard. "I don't believe we've met. I'm Declan Wilde."

"Of the famous Wilde family of London socialites?"

"Yes, that's me. My wife, Sabrina, is American." He glances at my bat, and I notice he holds one too. "Well, let's see who wins this match. Team Declan or Team Dominic?"

"Is that a cricket bat from the Jurassic period?" Reese asks, eyeing my equipment with undisguised humor.

I glance down at my old bat, "It's been in storage for years."

"It belongs in a museum," Declan says, not unkindly. "Here, try mine."

He hands me his gleaming new bat, the polished wood shining in the afternoon sun. The weight distribution is perfectly balanced like my old bat never was. I give it an experimental swing, muscle memory kicking in despite years away from the sport.

"That's more like it," Dominic nods approvingly. "Now you look like a proper cricketer."

I swallow another swig of whisky, and the liquid courage spreads through my limbs. "Right. Let's get on with it then."

Chapter Twenty-Six

Jennifer

Today's game might be just a casual match to help Fletcher get comfortable with cricket again, but it still makes me a touch uneasy. I don't want my husband to get injured. I've heard—from the American Wives Club gals—that this game can be wild. Emery told me not to worry. She's a lovely woman, and I trust what she said, though nothing will completely eradicate my worries.

Right now, I'm standing here alone near the grassy area.

But not for long.

Several women saunter up to me wearing warm smiles and curious expressions. I recognize a few faces from the whirlwind of introductions earlier, though I'm still struggling to keep everyone straight.

"Jennifer!" Emery calls out, her smile infectious as she approaches with three other women in tow. "We couldn't let you stand here alone, worrying about the boys and their testosterone-fueled antics."

A laugh snorts out of me despite my nerves. "Is it that obvious I'm worried?"

"Honey, you're wringing your hands like you're trying to start a fire," says a petite blonde with a distinct American accent. She extends her hand. "I'm Keely MacTaggart, by the way. Evan's wife."

"And I'm Rae MacTaggart," adds a woman with striking reddish-gold hair. "Iain's better half. Don't worry about the cricket match—these boys are all bark and no bite when it comes to actual violence."

The third woman, a brunette with kind eyes, steps forward. "I'm Chelsea Rigby, Dominic's wife. I know exactly how you're feeling. I was terrified the first time I watched him play after we got married."

Relief washes over me. "But you seemed so calm during introductions."

Chelsea laughs, tucking a strand of dark hair behind her ear. "Oh, I've had years to perfect my poker face. But inside? I'm still holding my breath every time he swings that bat."

"The key," Rae interjects with a wry smile, "is to focus on something else entirely. Like gossiping about our husbands' terrible cricket form."

"Ian's particularly dreadful," Chelsea continues. "Last time he played, he managed to hit the ball directly into his own wicket. I've never seen a Scotsman turn that shade of red."

I bite my lip. "Fletcher's been out of practice for years. I'm worried he'll hurt himself trying to impress everyone."

"Men," Keely says with a knowing nod. "They'd rather break a limb than admit they're rusty. But have you seen Declan play? Holy cow, that man is a machine on the pitch—and damn sexy too."

Sabrina Wilde, Declan's American Wife, trots up to us. "Sorry to tell you this, girls, but my honey's team is going to trounce Fletcher's guys."

Eye rolls accompany her statement.

I step in to save my man's reputation. "Fletcher is the Terminator. Nobody will knock him out of the match. He's one hot daddy."

Heidi Petrescu had hung back a bit, listening to our conversations, clearly amused by what the other wives had said. "Have you girls ever watched Damian deal cards for a reading? Now that's damn hot."

Emery links her arm around mine, guiding me toward a row of chairs set up under a large canopy. "Come sit with us. We've got comfy chairs and the best view of the pitch, not to mention emergency ice packs ready just in case."

I follow them, grateful for the company, and settle into a comfortable folding chair that has padding. *Nice.* Someone hands me a cold glass of lemonade, and I suddenly realize how thirsty I am.

"So," Rae begins, leaning toward me, "how are you adjusting to being Mrs. Murgatroyd? Four kids, brand-new husband, and now a houseful of international guests? I don't know how you do it. Two kids are enough for me."

I take a long sip of my lemonade, grateful for the cool liquid that soothes my suddenly dry throat. "It's been overwhelming at times, in the best possible way. The children have adjusted faster than I expected. I love them all so much."

"Children are resilient like that," Chelsea says with a knowing smile. "And from what I've heard, you were part of the family long before the wedding."

"True," I admit. "Though going from nanny to wife was quite the promotion."

My new friends laugh, and I realize I'm relaxing into their easy camaraderie. There's something comforting about being surrounded by women who understand exactly what it's like to be thrust into this whirlwind of British and Scottish traditions.

"Oh! They're starting!" Keely points toward the pitch where the men have formed into teams.

I lean forward in my chair, my heart rate picking up as I watch Fletcher position himself on the pitch. He seems confident holding that borrowed bat, despite the slight tension in his shoulders that suggests he's more nervous than he's letting on.

"That's my husband with the wickets," Emery says, pointing toward a tall man with dark hair who's setting up behind the stumps. "Rory's actually really good at this, though he'll never admit it. The MacTaggart men think shinty is the only true sport."

"Fletcher looks nervous," I admit, unable to tear my eyes away from my husband as he takes a few practice swings.

"They all do at first," Rae assures me, settling back in her chair with the ease of someone who's watched countless shinty matches. "But once they get into the rhythm of it, they become absolute children again. It's endearing, actually."

Chelsea nods in agreement. "Dominic transforms the minute his feet hit the pitch. One second he's my girls-school cricket coach husband, the next he's ten years old again, showing off for his friends."

I watch the men divide into teams, with Fletcher joining Dominic's side. They're laughing and jostling each other, passing around that whisky bottle like it's water. I hope he doesn't guzzle too much of Thane Buchanan's whisky.

"They've been drinking," I observe, trying to keep my voice neutral.

Keely snorts. "That's cricket tradition. Liquid courage. Don't worry—they're not really drunk. Yet."

Oh, great. I thought Fletcher would only take a swig to calm his nerves.

"First cricket match jitters," Emery tells me, patting my knee sympathetically. "We've all been there."

Another woman approaches our group, and Emery leaps out of her chair to sling an arm around the newcomer. "Ladies! Look who finally showed up. It's Ashley Murdoch. I don't think you've met Jennifer yet, have you?"

Ashley Murdoch turns out to be a warm, friendly American woman with an infectious smile. Her brown hair is pulled back in a practical ponytail, and she's wearing comfortable, casual clothing that immediately puts me at ease.

"Jennifer! I'm so sorry I'm late," Ashley says, giving me a quick hug like we're old friends. "I got caught up helping wrangle some of the younger kids. Your Henry is quite the little explorer, isn't he?"

My heart skips a beat. "What did he do now?"

"Nothing much," Ashley quickly reassures me with a laugh. "He just convinced three other children that they could build a fort out of cricket equipment. I found them constructing what they called a 'cricket castle' using stumps and protective pads."

"That sounds like Henry," I sigh. "He has a gift for turning any situation into an adventure."

"He'll fit right in with Lucas," Ashley declares. "He's a little adventurer too, just like his daddy."

Once we've all settled down again in our chairs, the practice game begins. Fletcher is on Dominic Rigby's team. Declan Wilde helms the opposing team.

First up is Errol Murdoch.

The Scot they call the fire starter whacks that ball like it's lit on fire and launches himself several feet into the air before smacking down onto the grass again. And then he whoops. Loudly.

Jeez, I pray he's the only one who plays cricket like that.

I'm not the only one who gasped as Errol's feet left the ground. The man seems to hang midair for an impossible moment before crashing back to earth with a triumphant shout. Fletcher stares at him with wide eyes, and I can practically read his thoughts: *Am I supposed to do that?*

"Is that…normal?" I ask weakly, clutching my lemonade like it might protect me from witnessing my husband's attempt to perform similar acrobatics.

Rae pats my arm reassuringly. "That's just Errol showing off. Most of these men haven't played properly in years. They're just here to have fun and relive their glory days."

"Errol always was the dramatic one," Chelsea adds with a fond eye roll. "Emery says he was crazy like that. All flash, no subtlety, but plenty of heart."

I watch as Fletcher takes his position at the crease, his posture shifting into something more confident, more familiar. Despite his years away from the game, there's muscle memory at work. He squares his shoulders, plants his feet just so, and raises the bat with a fluid motion.

"Look at that stance," Chelsea murmurs appreciatively beside me. "Your husband hasn't forgotten a thing."

The bowler—I think it's Chance Dixon—charges forward with surprising speed for a man his age. The ball flies from his hand in a blur of red. My heart leaps into my throat as it hurtles toward Fletcher.

Then—crack!—the sweet sound of bat meeting ball echoes across the field. Fletcher connects with a powerful swing that sends the ball soaring. The men whoop and holler as he takes off running.

"Go, Fletcher!" I shout, leaping out my chair to whistle and wave my arms in the air.

Yeah, I think my hubby will do just fine tomorrow.

Chapter Twenty-Seven

Fletcher

On this warm and lovely day in Millbrook Valley, Nebraska, the apocalypse has finally arrived. I expect to see demons pouring out of the heavens at any moment. Maybe I had performed reasonably well on the pitch yesterday, but that was a practice game. The shot of Thane's whisky those tossers gave me yesterday has worn off this afternoon. Dominic suggested I should try another swig of that elixir, but I declined. If I'm going to die today, I might as well be sober.

The players for this match have jogged onto the field. All except me, that is.

Dominic slaps my arm as he hurries past me. "Time to crush the competition, eh, Fletch?"

"Are you out of your mind, you demented bastard?"

Errol Murdoch halts beside me, grinning. "Dinnae fash, mate. You've got the fire starter on your side, not to mention Damian the fortune teller and all three Dixon laddies. We cannae lose!"

If you say so, you raging lunatic.

I do like Errol, but his manner of playing cricket is…unusual, to say the least.

The moment I've reached my position on the pitch, I begin to sweat. The sun blazes down on us, and I wonder if I can fake a sudden bout of food poisoning to escape this ordeal. Jennifer waves from the sidelines, surrounded by the American Wives Club. Even from here, I can see the encouraging smile on her face. I'd hate to disappoint my bride by making a complete arse of myself.

"All right there, Murgatroyd?" Declan shouts from across the field while tossing a cricket ball from hand to hand with infuriating ease. "You look like you're about to faint."

"Sod off, you wanker. I'm bloody fantastic," I lie, wiping my forehead with the back of my hand. "I'm contemplating your team's imminent defeat."

At the periphery of the pitch, I see my family. Henry jumps up and down shouting, "My dad's going to win! Nobody else can beat him!"

I can't resist grinning and chuckling at my youngest son's enthusiasm. What if I let my family down by cocking up this match? No, I could never do that. I'll win this death match for my children.

"Get ready, gentlemen," shouts the umpire, Dane Dixon, who volunteered for duty and seems far too calm about the whole affair. Cricket can be hazardous, after all. "Let's have a proper, gentlemanly match!"

"Since when is cricket gentlemanly?" Damian Petrescu hollers while smirking.

I ignore him and take my position at the crease, gripping Declan's borrowed bat like it's a life preserver. We're on opposite teams, yet he made sure I had a good bat. The weight feels foreign in my hands despite yesterday's practice. My palms are slick with sweat too, and every pair of eyes on the field remains focused on me.

Rory MacTaggart takes the ball for the opposing team, rolling it between his massive hands with the casual confidence of a man who played at university level—but I've heard he never played the sport until recently. The Scot is built like a bloody tree trunk, all shoulders and arms that could probably launch a cricket ball into orbit.

I swallow hard as Rory settles into his bowling position. When he begins his run-up, I swear the ground trembles beneath my feet.

"You've got this, Fletcher!" Jennifer's voice cuts through the havoc of my thoughts. "Massacre the enemy, baby! I want that grass to turn red!"

When did my wife become a bloodthirsty maniac? Oddly, that turns me on.

I adjust my grip on the bat, willing my sweaty palms to co-operate. The borrowed cricket whites are stiff and unfamiliar. I haven't played a proper match since university.

"Focus on the ball," Dominic reminds me from the sidelines. "Not on MacTaggart's intimidating Scottish scowl!"

Easy for him to say. Dom isn't the one about to be humiliated in front of his entire family. Which MacTaggart was he talking about, anyway? There are several on the pitch.

Rory charges forward, his arm windmilling with terrifying precision. The red ball shoots from his hand like a crimson blur. Time slows to a crawl as I track its trajectory, my heart hammering against my ribs. The ball spins wickedly through the air, heading straight for my middle stump. Everything my father taught me about cricket floods back to me in an instant.

Keep your eye on the ball. Stay balanced. Don't overthink it.

I swing.

That sweet spot connects flawlessly, sending vibrations up my arms as the ball rockets away from me in a beautiful arc. Holy shit, I actually hit it. Hard.

"Run!" Dominic roars from behind the wickets, and my legs finally remember how to move.

I sprint toward the opposite crease, my heart soaring as I hear the crowd erupting in cheers. Henry's voice rises above the rest as he screams my name with sheer childlike joy as I pound across the pitch. Adrenaline is pumping through my veins as the crowd's roar nearly deafens me. The grass blurs beneath my feet, and for a moment I feel like I'm twenty years old again, invincible and alive with the pure joy of the game.

"Yes!" I hear Errol shout from somewhere behind me. "That's how it's done, Fletcher!"

I reach the crease just as the wicketkeeper collects the ball, and I'm breathing so hard that I can't speak. I'm grinning like an absolute madman. The fielders are still chasing my shot toward the boundary, and I realize with dawning amazement that I might have hit a four.

"Bloody brilliant!" Dominic shouts. "You've still got it, mate!"

I turn toward the sidelines, searching for Jennifer's face in the crowd. When I spot her, she's on her feet, jumping up and down like a woman possessed, waving a makeshift banner that I'm fairly certain she fashioned from someone's jacket.

"That's my husband!" she screams at the top of her lungs, completely abandoning any pretense of dignified spectating. "Fletcher Ralph Murgatroyd, you rock!"

My feet must have lifted off the ground, weightless. It feels that way right now, at least. The terror that gripped me moments ago has transformed into pure exhilaration. I *can* do this.

The next ball comes faster than the first, spinning wickedly as it bounces off the pitch. This time I'm ready for it. My stance feels natural now as muscle memory overrides years of rust. I step forward, meeting the ball with a confident drive that sends it skimming along the ground toward the boundary.

"Two runs!" the umpire calls as I sprint again.

I pump my legs harder, every breath coming in sharp bursts as I make the turn and sprint back to my original crease. The fielders are scrambling, but I can see the ball's still a good distance from the wickets.

"Come on, Dad!"

I hear Charlotte screaming from the crowd.

"Don't let them catch you!"

My gaze flicks to Amelia, who's also screaming and pumping her fists in the air. "Go, Dad! Whup those jerks!"

The wicketkeeper is positioned perfectly, gloves ready, but the throw from the boundary comes in just wide of his reach. I slide into the crease with inches to spare, my whites now decorated with grass stains that I'll wear like badges of honor.

Six runs from two balls. Not bad for a rusty old father of four.

"Show off," Declan mutters from behind me. But it's obvious he's teasing me.

As the game goes on, I manage another boundary, then a solid defensive block against a particularly nasty delivery from Thane Buchanan.

I glance over at Jennifer between balls. She's leaning forward in her seat, totally absorbed in the match. The other wives have draped an arm around her shoulders, and they're all cheering like maniacs. I feel ten feet tall just from knowing she's here, watching.

By the time our side is bowled out, I've managed to score twenty-eight runs. Not spectacular by any means, but respectable enough that I can hold my head high. The children are beside themselves with excitement as I jog off the pitch.

"Dad!" Henry launches himself at my legs. "You were amazing! Like a superhero but with a bat!"

I ruffle his hair. "Thanks, champ. I had a good teacher in your grandfather."

"Did you see me watching?" Charlotte asks, her eyes wide. "I didn't look away once, even when Amelia tried to distract me with candy."

"I did no such thing."

Now it's time to bowl again, and I'm batting the last delivery of the over. Declan glances my way, winks, and takes his position. I grip the bat tighter. This is it. The final ball of our innings. Everything comes down to this moment. The crowd has gone eerily quiet, but I'm not anxious. No, I'm reveling in the heat of the game.

Declan begins his run-up, his face a mask of determination.

Despite us being on opposite teams, there's something almost ceremonial about this moment between us. Two British blokes reliving their youth through leather and willow.

The ball leaves his hand in a perfect arc, spinning just enough to catch the afternoon light. I watch it bounce once on the pitch, then rise toward me with deceptive speed. My body moves without conscious thought, stepping into the shot, rotating my hips, bringing the bat around in a smooth, controlled swing.

Contact.

The sound is different this time—cleaner, more resonant. The ball rockets off my bat with a satisfying thwack, sailing high over the heads of the fielders. I drop the bat and run like my life depends on it.

"Six!" Dane Dixon shouts from behind the stumps, and the crowd explodes.

I can barely hear anything over the roar of approval from my mates and my family. My legs feel like jelly as I complete the run, but I'm grinning so hard my cheeks ache. A six! I bloody well hit a six on the final ball!

Jennifer is screaming my name from the sidelines while jumping up and down. The American Wives Club women are all on their feet, cheering as if I've just won the World Cup.

"Fletcher! Fletcher! Fletcher!" Henry chants, his small voice carrying across the pitch as Josh joins in the chant along with Charlotte and Amelia.

My teammates rush toward me, whooping and hollering. Errol reaches me first, grabbing me in a bear hug that nearly lifts me off my feet. And somehow, I wind up on sitting on top of Dominic's shoulders.

"Fletcher Murgatroyd, you absolute legend!" he shouts, spinning round and round. "Did you see that ball fly? It's probably still traveling! Thirty-four runs, mate. You've earned your legendary status!"

Jennifer finally catches up to me, pushing through the pile of sweaty men to get there. Dom leans over so I can slide off his shoulders. My bride flings her arms around my neck, lifts herself onto her tiptoes, and kisses me with so deeply that it's that's almost indecent. My teammates whistle and whoop and cheer, but all the noise fades away as hoist Jennifer off her feet for an even deeper kiss.

The best part of all is that my kids think I'm a superhero. Yeah, I can live with that.

Chapter Twenty-Eight

Jennifer

I'm so proud of Fletcher for letting go of his fears and becoming the cricket hero he once had been. His ex-wife clearly treated him like garbage, and he became so downtrodden that he gave up on ever finding real happiness. On our wedding night, between bouts of hot sex, Fletcher had confessed to me that he'd allowed his ex, Claudia, to trample him emotionally.

These days, he's a rock star—to me, the kids, his friends, and everyone else who knows him. Fletcher's employees at the hotel already loved him. But once we showed them the videos of the cricket match, they now agree with me that Fletcher Murgatroyd is an extraordinary man.

He walks with a spring in his step these days and literally whistles while he works. The transformation has been astonishing, especially in the bedroom. I never expected my husband to become a sex god—but he has. And whoa mama, I love this new side of him.

A week after the cricket match, Fletcher and I take the kids and the grandparents as well as my parents too, on an end-of-summer escapade. We let the children suggest some destinations. That might not have been our smartest idea ever. Four kids arguing over what is the "awesome-est" vacation spot. After two hours of listening to the kids bicker over destinations, Fletcher finally steps in. His newfound confidence shines through as he claps his hands once, silencing the bedlam.

"Listen up, I've made an executive decision," he announces. "We're going to the Black Hills of South Dakota."

I bite back a laugh at the kids' stunned faces. Henry recovers first.

"But Dad, what about the water park I wanted?" His bottom lip quivers melodramatically.

Fletcher crouches to his level. "The park will still be there next summer, champ. But how many of your friends can say they've seen Mount Rushmore?"

Charlotte perks up. "Don't they have wild horses there too?"

"And the Badlands," Josh adds, already pulling out his tablet to research the sights. "Did you know they've found fossils there that are over 75 million years old?"

Amelia glances up from her phone, suddenly interested. "The Badlands? Isn't that where they filmed that movie about the alien crash site?"

"You're thinking of Area 51, genius," Josh says with an eye roll. "That's in Nevada."

"No bickering," Fletcher says firmly. "This vacation is about family bonding."

I wrap my arm around his waist, loving this take-charge version of my husband. "The Black Hills will be perfect. We can see Mount Rushmore, Crazy Horse Memorial, and explore Custer State Park."

"Will there be ice cream?" Henry asks, his priorities clearly established. To Henry, everything boils down to ice cream.

"Of course there will be ice cream," Fletcher assures Henry, ruffling his hair. "What kind of vacation doesn't have that?"

Just like that, the decision is made. I watch as the kids scatter to research South Dakota on their devices, already planning what they want to see. Fletcher's parents exchange amused glances with mine.

"Well, that was easier than expected," I tell Fletcher.

He kisses my temple. "Cricket hero, remember? I'm invincible now."

I laugh and nudge him with my hip. "Don't let it go to your head, Mr. Murgatroyd."

Two weeks later, we're packed into our rented van, heading north toward South Dakota. The grandparents, all six of them, follow in their own vehicle. That's probably for the best. Eight hours with six adults and four children in one van would test even Fletcher's newfound self-assurance.

My parents, Larry and Joanne Cordell, are thrilled to be invited on this excursion.

"Are we there yet?" Henry asks for the third time in thirty minutes.

"Not even close, buddy," I reply, passing him another snack bag. "We've only been on the road for two hours."

"But that's forever!" Henry whines, slumping in his seat while pouting.

"Try looking out the window," I suggest. "Count how many red cars you see. First one to twenty wins."

My plan distracts him for all of five minutes before he's fidgeting again. I glance at Fletcher, who's driving with one hand on the wheel, seeming completely unfazed by the shenanigans in the back seat. How does he do it? The man is unflappable these days.

"I need to pee," Charlotte announces abruptly.

"We just stopped twenty minutes ago," Fletcher reminds her, catching her eye in the rearview mirror.

"I didn't have to go then. But I do now."

Fletcher sighs but nods. "Next rest stop, then."

I squeeze his knee and whisper, "You're doing great."

He flashes me a crooked smile, the kind that still makes me weak in the knees. Even with four bickering kids in the back, I still take a moment to admire how handsome he is behind the wheel, so confident and relaxed.

"You know," I whisper so the kids can't hear, "watching you take charge like this is really doing it for me."

Fletcher's eyebrows shoot up, and he throws me a heated sideways glance. "Is that right, darling? Perhaps we'll need to find some alone time at the hotel."

"Count on it." I delicately trail my fingertips over his forearm.

The rest stop appears like an oasis on the horizon. As soon as Fletcher parks, Charlotte bolts from the van like she's been shot from a cannon. Henry follows, claiming he needs to pee too, though

I suspect he's more interested in the vending machines. Josh and Amelia stretch their legs, looking grateful to escape the confines of the van. I watch through the windshield as the grandparents' car pulls up beside us, all six of them appearing remarkably cheerful for people who've been driving for hours.

"Ten minutes," Fletcher calls out as the kids scatter toward the rest stop building. "And stay where I can see you!"

I climb out of the van, stretching my arms above my head. The summer air is warm but carries a hint of the cooler weather that's coming. Fletcher saunters up beside me, wrapping his arms around my waist from behind. "Halfway there, Jennifer."

"Thank heavens." I lean back against his chest, savoring this moment of peace. "Think we'll survive the rest of the trip?"

"With our sanity intact?" He smirks. "It's doubtful."

Fortunately, we do survive all three rest stops that we see along the way without losing anyone. And finally, we're we've reached our hotel. Everyone waits in their vehicles while Big Daddy gets us checked in. Fletcher returns a few minutes later, waving for us to exit our vehicles.

Within fifteen minutes, everyone has found their correct rooms—the grandparents, the kids, and also Fletcher and me. The boys have their own room, just like the girls do. Miraculously, none of the children complain. They even go to sleep within ten minutes of bedding down.

Now, Fletcher and I finally get some time alone in our room. But we're too exhausted to make love. Instead, we cuddle.

And promptly fall asleep.

In the morning, everyone is refreshed and ready to explore the Badlands. The starkly beautiful landscape stretches out before us like something from another planet. Red rock formations jut up from the earth in impossible shapes, carved by millions of years of wind and water into a landscape that seems more suited to Mars than South Dakota.

Henry presses his face against the window. "Whoa. This is so cool! It looks like where aliens would live."

"That's exactly what I was thinking," I agree, craning my neck to take in the towering spires of rock. "It's like we've driven into a science fiction movie."

Fletcher pulls into the visitor center parking lot, and I can tell he's as impressed as the rest of us. His whole expression changes as he surveys the dramatic landscape stretching toward the horizon.

"Right then," he says, turning off the engine. "Everyone ready to explore?"

The kids practically tumble out of the van in their excitement. Josh immediately starts rattling off geological facts about sedimentary rock formations that he must've memorized. Charlotte immediately starts planning the best photo spots now that her dad bought her a camera. We had nixed the idea of letting our kids sign up on any social media site. A camera is the next best thing.

"Did you know," Josh announces to anyone within earshot, "that these formations are called 'badlands' because early settlers thought the terrain was too hard to cross?"

Amelia rolls her eyes. "Fascinating."

Despite her seeming disinterest, I catch Amelia snapping a photo of the dramatic rock spires.

The grandparents emerge from their rental van looking surprisingly spry despite the long journey. My dad immediately starts pointing out geological features to Fletcher's father, while the moms huddle together, probably mapping out our itinerary down to the minute.

"Look at that formation over there," Fletcher says, pointing toward a particularly striking red and white striped cliff. "It's like layers of history written in stone."

I love watching him get excited about things like this. The cricket match really did unlock something in him. He's confident, virile, cheerful, and focused on our children more than ever before.

"Can we hike one of those trails?" Charlotte asks, bouncing on her toes as she studies the visitor center map.

"Yes, why not?" Fletcher replies. "But we stick together as a group. No wandering off."

Josh already has his nose buried in a park brochure. "What about the fossil trail? It says here that you can see actual prehistoric remains embedded in the rock."

Henry's eyes go wide. "Like dinosaur bones?"

"More like ancient sea creatures," Josh explains with the patience of someone who genuinely loves sharing knowledge. "This whole area used to be underwater millions of years ago."

I watch Fletcher absorb this information, nodding thoughtfully. Six months ago, he would have been checking his watch or suggesting we skip ahead to the next attraction. Now he's immersed in the moment, genuinely curious about the natural wonders around us.

The change in him is unmistakable—and wonderful.

Chapter Twenty-Nine

Fletcher

Our last day in the Badlands takes us to an unusual, intriguing location called Wall Drug, a sprawling tourist attraction that we've heard has become a legend in its own right. I've been seeing billboards for this place for the last hundred miles, each one more outrageous than the last. *Free Ice Water at Wall Drug!* And, *Only 50 Miles to Wall Drug!* The children have been counting them like some sort of bizarre road trip bingo game.

As we pull into the parking lot, I find myself grinning at the sheer audacity of the place. Wall Drug sprawls across what looks like several city blocks, a maze of wooden storefronts designed to look like an Old West town. The whole thing is delightfully kitschy, and I can already see the children's eyes lighting up. Even Jennifer seems entranced by the eccentric atmosphere.

"This is crazy," my wife whispers beside me, but she's smiling as she says it. "How did a pharmacy in the middle of nowhere become this massive tourist destination?"

"Marketing genius," I reply, watching as Henry presses his face against the van window. "Free ice water during the Great Depression, then they just kept adding attractions until it became this wonderland of American roadside culture."

"Says an Englishman. You Brits must have your own wacky destinations too, though."

"Oh yes, indeed we do." I wag my eyebrows at her. "We've got Stonehenge, which is essentially a pile of rocks that people travel thousands of miles to see. And don't get me started on the various museums dedicated to cheese-rolling or Morris dancing. I can't forget the Gnome Reserve in Devon either, where hundreds of garden gnomes live in a woodland setting. Visitors are encouraged to wear pointy red hats to make the gnomes feel comfortable."

Jennifer laughs, linking her arm through mine as we exit the van. "I'd love to see those someday. Maybe that should be our next family vacation—showing the kids your homeland."

"They would love it. Henry would go mad for the Tower of London—all those gruesome execution stories."

Henry rushes up to me. "Dad! They have a giant dinosaur! Come on!"

Sure enough, there's an enormous T-Rex model roaring mechanically at passing tourists. Henry stands beneath it, arms outstretched in a matching "roar" pose while Charlotte snaps photos.

I whistle to get the kids' attention. "Five-minute rule. No one wanders off beyond my line of sight." I point to the entrance. "We meet back at this spot in an hour if we get separated."

"An hour?" Amelia groans, already eyeing a shop displaying turquoise jewelry. "Dad, there's like a million things to see in there."

"One hour, love. No more."

The grandparents have already disappeared inside, lured by promises of homemade fudge and five-cent coffee.

Jennifer squeezes my hand. "Ready to embrace American kitsch culture?"

I make a grand gesture with one arm. "Lead the way, milady."

Once we're inside, Wall Drug is even more chaotic than I'd imagined. The place is a labyrinth of interconnected shops, each one more bizarre than the last. Every corner reveals some new oddity—a mechanical piano playing ragtime, a towering case of jackalopes, and what appears to be a life-sized cowboy band that springs to animation when someone drops a quarter in the slot.

"Dad, can I have a quarter?" Josh appears at my elbow, pointing to the animatronic display. "I want to see how it works."

I dig into my pocket for change. "Here you go. Engineering research, is it?"

He grins, already analyzing the mechanism. "The gears must be connected to a timing belt that coordinates the movements. I bet there's a hidden air compressor too."

Jennifer slips her hand into mine as we watch Josh carefully deposit the coin. The cowboy band jerks to life with a wheezing rendition of "Home on the Range" that makes Henry double over with laughter. "This place is fun. Don't you think so, Fletcher?"

"It is beginning to grow on me."

We spend the next hour exploring every nook and cranny of Wall Drug, and I'm genuinely charmed by the place's unabashed commitment to tourist trap excellence. The children scatter like marbles, each drawn to different attractions. Henry discovers a penny-stretching machine and becomes obsessed with creating elongated Lincoln profiles.

I'm examining a display of vintage postcards when Amelia sidles up to me, looking unusually serious.

"Dad," she says quietly, "can we talk for a minute?"

I freeze, not even blinking. Serious conversations with my eldest daughter rarely end well. "Yes, pet, we can do that. What's on your mind?"

She glances around, making sure we're out of earshot of the others. Then she flings her arms around me for a firm but brief hug. "I just wanted to say…thank you. For this vacation. For everything, really."

I blink, caught off guard by her earnest tone. "What do you mean, love?"

"Well, I mean…" She fidgets with the hem of her T-shirt, seeming younger than her fifteen years. "Before Jennifer came, we were all just, you know, happy enough but not as happy as we should've been. When Mom left, you were trying so hard but you were sad all the time."

My throat tightens. I hadn't realized how much my children had noticed during those dark months.

"But now you're different," Amelia continues, her voice gaining strength. "You laugh more. You actually want to do things with us instead of just checking items off some parental obligation list. Like this trip—the old you would have booked us into a boring educational museum and called it bonding time."

I let out a shaky laugh. "Wall Drug is hardly highbrow. And I'll have you know, I've always wanted to do fun things with you lot."

Amelia smiles shyly. "Sure, Dad. But you weren't having fun yourself. Now you are. It's…nice."

I'm momentarily speechless. My teenage daughter, who typically communicates through eye rolls and exaggerated sighs, is standing here having a genuine heart-to-heart with me. I pull her into another hug, not caring that we're in a touristy shop.

"Thank you, Amelia," I murmur into her hair. "That means more than you know."

She allows the hug for precisely three seconds before extracting herself with a dramatic, "Dad, people are watching."

"Let them watch."

After our exploration of the strangest drug store I've ever seen, it's time for our large extended family to get back on the road. Even the kids agree we should go straight home and only stop for breakfast, lunch, and dinner. If we keep to that schedule, we might be home by early afternoon.

The drive back to Millbrook Valley passes in a blur of prairie landscapes and sleepy children. Even Jennifer dozes against my shoulder for most of the journey, her hand resting on my thigh in that casual way married couples often develop. I steal glances at her while she sleeps, still amazed that this incredible woman chose me—chose us.

"Dad," Henry pipes up from the back seat, "when we get home, can we put all our pictures in a scrapbook?"

"That's a brilliant idea, champ." I catch his eager face in the rearview mirror. "We'll make a proper family album."

"I want to write captions for everything," Charlotte adds. "Like 'The Day Dad Conquered Wall Drug' and 'Henry Versus the Mechanical Dinosaur.'"

Even Josh tears himself away from his book. "We should include geological data about the rock formations we saw."

"What a clever idea."

We keep to the schedule I had suggested and arrive home by twelve forty-five. Before we can return to our house, though, first we need to drop off the grandparents as well as Jennifer's parents. Larry and Joanne opted to take a room at my hotel. Well, the hotel where I'm general manager. I don't own the place.

Finally, our little family pulls into the drive. Henry has already fallen asleep, so I carry him into the house and into the bedroom he shares with Josh.

Amelia yawns. "NGL I'm zonked."

I raise a brow. "And that means…"

"Not gonna lie. I'm really tired."

"You could take a nap, love."

Her jaw drops, and she stops blinking. "At two in the afternoon? I'm not super old like you and Jennifer."

I pretend to clutch my chest. "You wound me, my child."

She shakes her head. "Old people are sooo weird."

Despite her horror at my suggestion, Amelia does doze off on the sofa—beside Charlotte. Josh crashes on the floor.

After their respective naps, we eat an early dinner. And finally, the house is quiet again. Jennifer and I go to sleep not long after. But in the morning, we're all rejuvenated. Breakfast chatter centers on our fantastic vacation. I sip my coffee and watch as my children chatter excitedly about their favorite parts of the trip. Henry's animated description of the mechanical T-Rex has everyone laughing, his little hands mimicking the dinosaur's jerky movements.

Josh sidles up beside Charlotte. "Remember when Dad almost got pooped on by that bird at Mount Rushmore?"

Charlotte nearly spits out her orange juice. "Yuck! Boys are so gross."

"It wasn't 'almost,' Charlotte," I correct her with mock seriousness. "That blasted bird had perfect aim. Thank goodness for baseball caps."

As the laughter of four children and two adults fills the air, I realize I'm more contented than ever before. I claim Jennifer's winking at her furtively. She kisses my cheek.

The doorbell rings. Who on earth could that be?

"I'll get that." I push my chair back and rush to open the door. My jaw drops. "Claudia? What in the world are you doing here?"

"Visiting my children. What else?"

Chapter Thirty

Jennifer

I'm pretty sure my mouth is hanging wide open, far enough that a small squirrel could crawl in there. Did Fletcher just call that woman Claudia? As in his ex-wife? The one who ditched him for an Australian yoga instructor? And she moved to kangaroo-land with him? If I think any more question marks in my mind, my head might explode. I stare blankly at Claudia and her designer duds, while Fletcher seems to have lost the ability to speak or even close his mouth.

I put on my best cheerful smile, hoping to defuse this puzzling situation. Then I aim a subtler smile at the kids. "Why don't you guys go to your rooms and play, all right? The adults need to have a little chat."

The children exchange curious glances but obey.

Once they're out of earshot, I clasp Fletcher's hand while pulling him aside so I can shut the door for our two guests.

Claudia steps forward. "Thank you for letting me come into your lovely home, Fletcher. And who is this lovely woman beside you?"

"I'm Jennifer, Fletcher's wife."

She smiles brightly at my husband, then turns her attention back to me. Claudia's words and mannerisms strike me as genuine. "I'm Claudia Sullivan, and the wonderful man beside me is Marcus Blackwood. I'm so pleased to meet you, Jennifer. My mother let me know that I could find you and Fletcher here. She lives just down the street, doesn't she?"

"A few blocks down. Fletcher's parents live across the street from each other."

Fletcher squints at his ex-wife. "What are you doing here? You can't just show up after all these years and demand—"

"I haven't demanded anything. Please, give me a chance to explain."

Fletcher huffs. "About what? How you abandoned our children?"

"No, I…" Claudia takes a deep breath, threading her fingers between Marcus's. "I've changed since the last time we saw each other, and I've learned a lot about myself. For one thing, I stopped drinking five years ago."

"Am I meant to congratulate you?"

"No, of course not. I-I wanted to explain…" She clings to Marcus as if he's her life preserver. "Please, just listen—"

Fletcher scowls at her.

Before this can turn into a battle royal, I should intervene. So, I wrap my arm around Fletcher's biceps and give him a reassuring smile. "I think you should listen, honey, for the sake of the children. At least find out what their mother has to say before you go thermonuclear."

Fletcher tenses under my touch, and I can sense him relaxing slightly as he processes my words. "You have five minutes."

Claudia exhales, her shoulders dropping slightly. "Thank you."

I gesture toward the living room. "Why don't we sit down? I can make some tea or coffee."

"That's very kind, but we're fine," Marcus replies. He has kind eyes that crinkle at the corners—the sort of face that puts you instantly at ease, despite the awkward circumstances.

We move to the living room in an uncomfortable procession. Fletcher sits rigid and bolt upright beside me on the sofa, while Claudia and Marcus take the armchairs opposite us. The coffee table between us might as well be the Grand Canyon.

"I should start by saying I'm deeply sorry." Claudia's voice catches slightly. "I know those words can't begin to make up for what I did, but they're true. I abandoned my children, and I've regretted it every day since."

I glance at Fletcher, whose jaw is clenched so tight I worry he might crack a tooth. His knuckles have gone white where his hands grip his knees.

"I was a mess back then," Claudia continues. "The depression hit me hard. I convinced myself the kids would be better off without me. That Fletcher was the better parent, anyway."

Fletcher grunts. "At least That part was true."

I squeeze his hand, trying to keep him grounded. This is clearly excruciating for him.

"Just to be clear," Claudia says, "I was still struggling with depression after I moved to Australia. A great therapist helped me deal with those issues, though it took years to recover. I but Marcus is the hero who saved me with his love and compassion. At his suggestion, I came back to America to confront what I've done and—most importantly—to apologize to my children."

I study Claudia's face, searching for signs of deception, but all I see is genuine remorse. Her perfectly manicured hands tremble slightly as she speaks. Fletcher remains silent beside me, his breathing shallow and controlled.

"I don't expect forgiveness," she continues. "I don't deserve it. But I wanted my children to know that my leaving wasn't their fault. It was mine. All mine."

Marcus places a supportive hand on her knee. "Claudia has worked incredibly hard on her recovery. She talks about the children often."

"Recovery?" Fletcher's voice is dangerously quiet. "Is that what you call it? You deserted your family, ran off to Australia with your yoga instructor, and now you've 'recovered'? It's bollocks."

I lay a hand on his chest. "Please, let's all take a deep breath. Claudia, I understand you want to apologize to the children, but you need to understand that your arrival is quite a shock."

Marcus makes a pained face. "We should have called first. That was my suggestion, but Claudia was afraid you wouldn't agree to see her."

Fletcher narrows his gaze. "She was right."

Claudia leans forward, her designer bracelets jingling softly. "I know this is difficult, Fletcher. But I'm not here to disrupt your lives or try to take the children. I just want them to understand that leaving wasn't their fault."

"They already know that," I explain gently. "Fletcher worked very hard to help them understand that your choices weren't a reflection on them. He did that by himself, before I even met him."

Marcus whispers to Claudia, and she nods in agreement with whatever he told her. Then she looks at Fletcher. "Marcus and I will stay at a hotel for a few days in case you and Jennifer want to discuss the issue. No pressure, I promise."

Silence descends on us like an iron cloak. I guess none of us knows what to say.

"Does anybody care what we think?"

I watch as the adults freeze at the sound of Amelia's voice. My stepdaughter stands in the doorway, arms crossed, her face a perfect teenage mask of defiance. Behind her, Charlotte, Josh, and Henry peek out like curious meerkats.

Fletcher's eyebrows shoot up. "How long have you lot been standing there?"

"Long enough," Amelia says, stepping fully into the room. The other children follow, forming a protective cluster. "If you're going to talk about us, we should be part of the conversation."

I'm torn between pride at her courage and concern about the emotional bombshell that's about to drop. Fletcher looks like he might spontaneously combust.

"This is an adult discussion," he begins, but I touch his arm gently.

"They have a right to be heard," I whisper. "This affects them more than anyone."

Claudia's eyes widen as she sweeps her gaze over the four children standing in the doorway. She rises halfway from her seat, then seems to think better of it and sinks back down.

"Hello, my darlings," she says, her voice trembling slightly. "It's been such a long time, hasn't it?"

I watch Amelia's face harden at the term of endearment. Charlotte inches closer to her big sister, while Josh stares at his mother with scientific detachment, as if she's a specimen he's cataloging. Only Henry looks openly curious, his head tilted to one side.

"You're our mom?" Henry asks, stepping forward. "The one who went to Australia?"

Claudia nods, tears welling in her eyes. "Yes, sweetheart. I'm your biological mother. But I know Jennifer is your real mom, the one who takes care of you every day."

Her words hit me like a splash of cold water. Did she really just call me their "real mom"? The ache in my chest says she did. My eyes dart to Fletcher, who looks equally stunned by this unexpected acknowledgment.

Henry steps forward, his small face scrunched in confusion. "But you're our first mom?"

"Yes, that's right."

Amelia's posture remains rigid, her gaze narrowed. "You left us. You never even called."

"But she sent us cards and gifts for birthdays and holidays," Charlotte declares. "Didn't she, Dad?"

Fletcher aims a tight smile at his youngest daughter. "Yes, she did do that."

Henry tromps up to Claudia, tipping his head side to side as if he can't figure out what kind of species she is. "What should we call you? We already have a mom."

"Just call me Claudia. Would that be all right?"

Henry shrugs. "Sure, why not."

Marcus lays an arm around Claudia's shoulders. "We should go to our hotel and give everyone a chance to process everything." He hands Fletcher a business card that has his company logo on it, but on the other side, he scrawled a phone number. "Call anytime. No rush."

And just like that, our lives have changed.

Chapter Thirty-One

Fletcher

After today's events, we decide to treat the children to whatever they want for dinner this evening. That means chicken fingers for Henry, though his preferred choice was, of course, ice cream. I told him, "No, Henry. Real food only please. Dessert comes later."

He pouted briefly but then gave up the battle.

We've just walked into Lucio's Family Ristorante, the best pizza place in Millbrook Valley. The hostess, a woman with dark-red hair that has purple streaks in it, greets us with a wide smile. "Table for six?"

"Yes, that's right," I confirm, watching Jennifer herd the kids into a line.

The restaurant buzzes with Friday night energy—families laughing, waiters balancing trays of steaming food, the wood-fired oven crackling in the open kitchen. The familiar smell of garlic and tomato sauce makes my stomach growl.

"Dad, look!" Henry points to the arcade games near the back. "Can I have quarters? Please?"

"After dinner," Jennifer tells him before I can respond. "Let's get everyone fed first."

"Good idea." I am enormously grateful for her ability to maintain order when all I want to do is give in to Henry's pleading eyes. Something about the way Jennifer handles the children with such ease reminds of how lucky I am to have found a woman like her. She has a natural talent I lack.

"Fletcher?" Jennifer catches me staring.

"Sorry, just thinking about how good you are with them."

We follow the hostess through the bustling restaurant and settle into a large corner booth. The kids immediately grab the paper placemats and crayons, except for Amelia, who's busy texting under the table.

"No phones at dinner, pet," I remind her.

She rolls her eyes but complies with minimal huffing. It's a bloody miracle.

Jennifer slides in beside me, her arm brushing mine as she reaches for a menu. The scent of her wafts over me, and I suddenly need to adjust my crotch. She always smells like…woman. It's intoxicating.

"I can't believe how hungry I am this evening," my wife whispers to me. "It'll be fun when Claudia and Marcus visit us for Thanksgiving."

"Yes, I'm looking forward to it as well." I freeze, abruptly shocked by what I've just said. "Crikey. Can't believe I'm actually excited about seeing them both."

Jennifer laughs gently. "My, how our lives have changed. Your ex-wife is now a good friend to both of us, and the kids are happier than ever despite school starting in a few days."

"It's quite shocking, isn't it?"

She laughs again in her sweet way that always warms me up from the inside out.

After our celebratory meal at the pizzeria, the kids are unusually well-behaved, a rarity worth savoring. Even Henry hasn't tried to stick a straw up his nose yet.

"What are you thinking about?" Jennifer asks, nudging me with her shoulder.

"Just how completely normal this feels. Family dinner. No disasters. No one's thrown food either. Yet."

She tries not to laugh but snorts instead. "Don't jinx it, sweetie."

Our server appears, a college-aged lad with an impressive tattoo on his left arm. "Ready to order?"

Henry bounces in his seat. "Chicken fingers! With extra ketchup!"

The server jots it down. "Got it, little man." The server turns to me, pen poised. "And for you, sir?"

"I'll have the meat lover's pizza, medium." I glance at Jennifer. "Share with me?"

She nods, her eyes crinkling at the corners. "Perfect. And can we get a side of garlic knots for the table?"

Amelia pipes up without glancing away from her placemat. "I want the pesto pasta, no mushrooms."

Once everyone's ordered, I lean back in the booth, my arm naturally falling behind Jennifer. The weight of the day seems to lift in this moment of normalcy.

During the next few months, leading up to Thanksgiving, Claudia and Marcus invite us to their place in Los Angeles for an extended-family meal. That means three sets of grandparents will come with us too. Marcus does very well as a yoga instructor, thanks mostly to his YouTube channel, so he and Claudia have gone all out for this event—paying for airline tickets for the whole family and setting us up in a swanky hotel.

"It's incredibly generous of them," Jennifer says as we browse flights on my laptop. "Though I'm a bit nervous about all the grandparents meeting in such close quarters for an extended period."

I pat her thigh. "Don't worry, love. I suspect my mother will be comparing etiquette notes with your father the entire time."

"And my mother will be interrogating yours about her skincare routine."

Henry bounces onto the sofa between us, nearly upending the laptop. "Will there be a pool? Marcus said there might be a pool!"

"Yes, there's a pool," I confirm, ruffling his hair. "And the beach is just a short walk away."

He grins and jumps up and down. "Can we go surfing? Marcus promised to teach me!"

"We'll see," I hedge, which is parent code for 'absolutely not.' But I don't have the heart to crush his excitement just yet.

Our trip to Los Angeles flies by in a blur of beaches and tourist shops and palm trees. We're glad to go home, but we will miss Marcus and Claudia. Still, we can look forward to Thanksgiving with them. We Murgatroyds know how to turn holidays into unforgettable events.

Before I know it, Thanksgiving Day has arrived.

The table is crowded in the best way, and the room is filled with jokes and laughter. Claudia has somehow managed to transform our dining room into an Instagram-worthy autumn wonderland. Candles flicker in mason jars wrapped with twine, and a centerpiece of gourds, pinecones, and tiny white pumpkins trails down the middle of the table.

"This is gorgeous," Jennifer says, squeezing my hand under the table. "Claudia has really gone all out."

"I agree." We watch as Marcus carries in the first turkey on a massive platter. With a theatrical flourish, pronounces, "Behold! The bird of gratitude!"

My mother claps politely while Jennifer's father, a retired teacher with a Santa Claus-like laugh, seems as if he's still deciding whether Marcus is a proper adult or not.

Then the Aussie returns to the kitchen to bring in another huge turkey that's slightly larger than the first. He sets it down with another regal flourish.

"Daddy carved the turkey last year," Henry informs everyone loudly.

"And this year it's my turn," Marcus announces with a grin, wielding the carving knife with surprising dexterity. "Two turkeys for this growing family."

I catch Jennifer's eye across the table. We both know what's coming.

"Actually," Henry pipes up, "Dad made a mess. There was turkey everywhere! Even in Amelia's hair!"

Amelia shoots him a death glare. "That's not true. Dad just had a little accident with the electric carver."

"The thing went rogue," I explain. "Perfectly normal kitchen mishap."

Marcus laughs. "Well, I promise no roasted turkey will be harmed today."

My mother leans toward Jennifer's mother and whispers something that makes them both titter. I pretend not to notice.

Jennifer rescues me, sort of, and winks too. "Fletcher has many talents—but carving isn't one of them."

I reach for her hand and squeeze it. "Cruel, but fair, darling. I've never been good at carving meat."

The warmth and joy of family surrounds as Marcus expertly slices the turkey, serving juicy portions to everyone. Even Jennifer's father looks impressed, which is no small feat.

"So," Claudia drawls, passing the cranberry sauce, "any exciting news to share with everyone?"

My heart skips. Jennifer and I exchange a quick glance, having discussed whether today would be the right moment. Her slight nod gives me courage.

"Since you asked..." I clear my throat deliberately, aware of all eyes turning to me. "Jennifer and I do have some news."

The table falls silent. Henry freezes in mid-bite, his dinner roll forgotten, sensing the shift in atmosphere.

Jennifer grins. "We're expecting."

A collective gasp ripples around the table. My mother's hand flies to her chest. Jennifer's father drops his fork with a clatter.

"You're—" Claudia's eyes widen, then she breaks into a radiant smile. "Oh my goodness! That's fabulous news!"

"When will the little one arrive?" Marcus asks, grinning. He holds the carving knife suspended in mid-air.

"May," Jennifer confirms, her cheeks flushing pink. "We're due in May."

Amelia stares at us, her expression unreadable. I catch her eye, trying to gauge her reaction. This affects her more than anyone. After a moment, she shrieks. "I'm getting another sibling?!"

I lay my hand over hers. "Yes, pet. How do you feel about that?"

She considers the idea for a moment, holding her forkful of stuffing in midair. "As long as I don't have to change diapers."

"Don't worry, Amelia. We won't make you do that, though I'm sure you'll enjoy playing with your new sibling."

Later, after all our guests have returned to their respective homes—or hotel room, for Claudia and Marcus—we put the children to bed. Once we're back in our room, I hold my wife close and nuzzle her cheek. As she falls asleep, I think back on how lonely I'd been after Claudia divorced me, and how much my life has changed in such a short time span.

Yes, I am the luckiest bloke on earth.

Love the

Hot Brits

series?

Visit
AnnaDurand.com

to subscribe to her newsletter for
updates on forthcoming books in this series
plus exclusive content!

*A*nna Durand is a bestselling, multi-award-winning author of contemporary and paranormal romance. Her books have earned bestseller status on every major retailer and wonderful reviews from readers around the world. But that's the boring spiel. Here are the really cool things you want to know about Anna!

Born on Lackland Air Force Base in Texas, Anna grew up moving here, there, and everywhere thanks to her dad's job as an instructor pilot. She's lived in Texas (twice), Mississippi, California (twice), Michigan (twice), and Alaska—and now Ohio.

As for her writing, Anna has always invented stories in her head, but she didn't write them down until her teen years. Those first awful books went into the trash can a few years later, though she learned a lot from those stories. Eventually, she would pen her first romance novel, the paranormal romance Willpower, and she's never looked back since.

To get exclusive content, join Anna's Facebook group, Anna's Romance Addicts, or sign up for her newsletter.

Visit AnnaDurand.com to sign up.